MISSING

James Stewart

Published by

**MELROSE
BOOKS**

An Imprint of Melrose Press Limited
St Thomas Place, Ely
Cambridgeshire
CB7 4GG, UK
www.melrosebooks.co.uk

FIRST EDITION

Copyright © James Stewart 2018

The Author asserts his moral right to
be identified as the author of this work

Cover by Melrose Books

ISBN   **978-1-912333-93-6 Paperback**
      978-1-912333-94-3 ePub
      978-1-912333-95-0 Mobi

Printed and bound in Great Britain by:
Ashford Colour Press Ltd
Unit 600
Fareham Reach
Fareham Road
Gosport
PO13 0FW

Chapter 1

Fathima sat in her bedroom in Colombo, Sri Lanka, contemplating her future. She was seventeen and had just passed her exams with star grades. Her stepfather was encouraging her to follow in his footsteps and go to Peradeniya University.

Fathima was very conscious of how successful her stepfather had been. He had sailed through university with a first in philosophy, politics and economics and was now the Minister for Home Affairs in the Sri Lankan government.

Fathima was happy about going to university but not just yet. Several of her friends were due to go in the coming autumn but Fathima wanted to see more of the world first. She wanted to take what the Europeans call a 'gap year' but she couldn't decide what to do.

Her present intention was to go to the UK as she wanted to improve her English. She had achieved a star in English in her exams, but wanted to be fluent so that when she came out of university, hopefully with a good degree, the world would be her oyster. However, she hadn't decided what she wanted to read and that was one of the reasons why she didn't want to rush her decision.

She was so happy and although sometimes she couldn't understand why, when she thought about it, it was obvious. She had a very comfortable existence living in a smart area of Colombo with her stepfather. He couldn't be more considerate. She adored him.

Her mother had married him when Fathima was eight years old. The marriage had been happy to start with but, in time, it clearly wasn't working. Her mother drank too much and, on occasions, was an embarrassment to her stepfather who had tried his best to get her to behave. This led to continual arguments. Eventually, she upped and left, giving Fathima the choice of either going with her or staying with her stepfather. Much to Fathima's surprise, when she said she was happy to stay where she was because her friends were here, her boyfriend was here and she had been to school here, her stepfather said he was perfectly happy for her to live with him. With that, her mother packed her bags and left, for goodness only knows where.

That was two years ago. Fathima had changed her surname to that of her stepfather, so she was now Fathima Mylvaganam and, from then on, she called her stepfather dad.

Fathima had only heard from her mother on her birthday. She presumed her father, as he now was, supported his wife financially but he never talked about her.

Fathima decided she would ask her boyfriend what he thought about her going to the UK. She was due to meet him in town for lunch so she got her bag, strapped it on the back of her scooter and rode off into the centre of town.

She liked Colombo, with its pavement cafés. It was March and it was hot and humid, but she had got used to it. She liked to go to the seaside with her dad who was teaching her to windsurf. The beaches in Sri Lanka were so beautiful, in some cases stretching for miles and miles. She couldn't understand why it wasn't as popular a holiday destination as, say, the West Indies. Perhaps it was the flights from Europe taking thirteen hours and stopping en route in Dubai.

The cricket, however, was a big attraction. Her dad had taken her to several test matches at Galle. She had seen most of the great Sri Lankan batsmen. It was 2008 and Sri Lanka was playing India. She had accompanied her father, who had been allocated VIP seats in the pavilion. She loved the match.

Her father knew Mahela Jayawardene and he introduced her to Anil Kumble, the Indian captain.

She arrived at the coffee shop, parked her scooter and secured it with a chain, a necessity these days, and went in to meet her boyfriend. Geoffrey was English and they had been going out together for only a few months. She was very fond of him but was too young to be thinking about settling down with anyone. She was still a virgin and wanted to remain that way until she got married.

Geoffrey was waiting for her: 'Coffee?' he asked.

'Yes, please, but I'll pay.'

'Okay, if you insist,' he replied.

They sat inside where there was air-conditioning as it was quite hot outside. They spoke in English, which was the second language for most educated Sir Lankans and it improved her English to have an English boyfriend.

'I've decided to take a year out and go to Europe,' she said.

'To do what?' asked Geoffrey.

'I haven't decided yet. I've thought about applying for a job as a chalet girl at a ski resort in Switzerland. A friend has done that but most of the people she meets are either Russian or German so that's not helping her with her English.'

'What about going to England as an au pair for a year? My parents had an au pair and if your charge is older than eight, they are far easier to manage than a baby and you can see more of the country with a child that age.'

'That's a good idea. I'll speak to my father about it.'

'But what about us?' asked Geoffrey.

'Well, you'll still be here in a year but you may have found someone else by the time I come back.'

He looked very sad.

Fathima broached the subject with her father that same

evening. He was always late home from work and this was no exception. It was about 8:00 pm.

'I think I'd like to go to the UK for a year as an au pair. What do you think?'

'I think it's a good idea but you'll have to find a suitable family.'

'Well, there are agencies here which specialise in au pair work. I'm sure I can find one.'

'You've got to be aware of the security angle, being my daughter.'

'I know,' she said. 'But I'll be very inconspicuous and very discreet.'

'I know that, Fathima, but it will be the first time you've been out of my sight.'

'Don't worry, Dad, I'll be fine,' she assured him.

* * *

The following morning, by pure chance, or so it seemed, a letter arrived for her father from a highly respected au pair agency. It read:

Dear Sir,

We understand your daughter is Fathima Mylvaganam. She has been identified as an ideal au pair for a Sri Lankan family living in the UK. They have a ten-year-old son who needs to be looked after while his mother and father are working. They are a highly-respectable family.

The family comprises Chaminda and Tanoo Jayasuriya and their son, Venkat. They live in the village of Baildon in West Yorkshire. Chaminda is a doctor and demonstrator in anatomy at Leeds University.

This, in our view, would be a highly desirable placement.
With kind regards,
Yours faithfully,
The Prestigious Au Pair Agency

Her father read the letter at breakfast.

'What do you think?' he asked. 'I'm sorry to be a damp squib, but the coincidence seems too good to be true.'

'Dad, you're always suspicious. Why not accept it for what it is? A super offer just when I'm looking for a job as an au pair.'

'That's what worries me,' he replied. 'I'll have him and the agency checked out, then we can take it from there. We'll talk about it later.'

What the hell, thought Fathima, *if it doesn't work out, I can find another family.*

* * *

Two days later, at the breakfast table, her father said: 'I've had the family checked out. They're just as the agency said, very respectable, so I can't see anything to stop you from taking the job. Get in touch with the agency, tell them you'll take the job and make sure you get all the necessary paperwork. Then let me know when you are going.'

'Oh, Dad, thanks,' said Fathima as she threw her arms around him.

'I've decided to do three things for you,' he said. 'First, to throw a party for you. You choose whichever restaurant you want. I put a limit on twelve, including you and me. I'm sure you'll want to invite your usual crowd.

'Second, once we know the date you're going, I'll organize

an open return flight with Emirates. I've managed to call in a few favours and can upgrade you from economy to business class.

'And, third, I've got the details of Barclays Bank in Baildon and once you are on your way, I'll deposit two thousand pounds in an account in your name. Then, if you get homesick, you can fly home whenever you want and you'll have some money in a local account to ensure you have the best of times.'

'That's fantastic, Dad, thank you so much. I'll try not to use it and live off my income. I don't want to take advantage of you.

'Bless you, Fathima,' he said. 'You'd never do that. I know you only too well. I'll miss you.'

* * *

Within days, Fathima had decided that she'd like her party to be at the Harbour Room restaurant at the Grand Oriental Hotel. The restaurant overlooked the bustling Colombo harbour and city and the food was amazing. She was going to choose the menu but because there were only twelve of them, the maître d' suggested they chose from the à la carte menu.

Fathima hoped this wasn't too extravagant but her father was very happy with her choice of restaurant, so she had his secretary book it. She was always good at that sort of thing and arranged a discreet quiet corner of the restaurant overlooking the harbour. The maître d' knew very well who had booked the table.

Fathima invited ten friends who were only too delighted to attend. They had a magnificent meal during which they chatted and laughed a lot and then her father tapped his glass.

'Friends,' he said quietly. 'This is a sad day for many of

us, but a happy one for Fathima. She will be away from us for a year, but we wish her the best of luck. Please keep in touch with her through Facebook. We all love her and wish her bon voyage.'

They all raised their glasses to a tearful Fathima.

The following day, as she settled down in her business class seat, Fathima couldn't believe her luck but as the plane rose from Colombo Airport, she wondered what she had let herself in for.

Chapter 2

Chaminda, Tanoo and Venkat Jayasuriya were waiting at Shipley Station for the five o'clock train from Leeds. They were there to meet Fathima, the au pair they had hired to look after Venkat, their son.

It was a cold and wet March afternoon and the shelter on the station platform was leaking. They had forgotten their umbrella and were cold, stamping their feet on the wet flagstones to try to keep warm. Chaminda and Tanoo had left work early, and had collected Venkat from school, so that they could all be there to welcome Fathima.

Fathima had flown into Heathrow from Sri Lanka and had telephoned to say she would be catching the train to Leeds and then to Shipley. She offered to take a taxi to their house but they knew she would be tired after her long journey and would, no doubt, have more than just one suitcase so they insisted on meeting her at the station.

The Jayasuriyas had hired her through an agency in Sri Lanka. All they knew about her was that her name was Fathima Mylvaganam and that she was seventeen years old. She was to look after their ten-year-old son, Venkat, and to help in the house. They had been impressed by her smiling photograph and the fact that she had a good command of the English language for a girl her age and was keen to improve it. They had been assured that she came from a good family.

The Leeds train slowly pulled into the station. A few passengers alighted, none of whom could be Fathima, and then a plumpish girl with haversack on her back, struggling with a large suitcase, stepped off the train onto the platform. She was wearing a waterproof jacket, jeans and shoes that were totally inadequate for the wet weather. She had a chubby, smiley face with some facial hair but no make-up and she looked younger than her seventeen years.

Tears came into Chaminda's eyes as he, Tanoo and Venkat walked quickly towards her to welcome her and help her with her suitcase.

'You must be Fathima,' said Tanoo.

'Yes,' she replied as Tanoo gave her a hug.

'Welcome to Yorkshire, Fathima. This is my husband, Chaminda, and our son, Venkat,' said Tanoo.

'Hello, I am pleased to meet you all,' said Fathima.

'The weather's not always like this,' said Tanoo. 'The car's parked nearby and we'll soon be home where I've got a nice supper waiting for you.'

They spoke in English as this was the understanding with the agency. Always speak English.

Fathima looked shy and uncertain but soon opened up after Tanoo and Chaminda's warm welcome. Venkat was very quiet.

It continued to rain as they drove to their home, a bungalow on Forest Hill in nearby Baildon. They lived in a pleasant cul-de-sac about ten minutes' walk away from the centre of Baildon village.

Fathima looked apprehensive. She said she'd never been outside Sri Lanka before. It was always hot there. Was she wondering what she'd let herself in for?

Once they had unloaded the car and were in the house, Tanoo said, 'Let me show you to your room. It has a nice view of Shipley Glen and you have your own shower room en suite, so I hope you will be comfortable. If you want a bath, you may use the house bathroom.'

'What a lovely house,' said Fathima. 'Thank you, the room

is very pretty. I think I'm going to like it here. You said it has a nice view?'

'Yes, a lovely view,' said Tanoo. 'You can see Shipley Glen where there used to be a small fairground with dodgem cars, booths and a historic aerial glide suspended roller-coaster, but that's gone now and all that's left is the Glen Tramway, a railway carrying people to and from Roberts Park in Saltaire. That would be a nice thing for you and Venkat to do on a fine day.'

Noticing that Fathima looked a little tense, she said, 'Don't worry. You'll be fine. Do you want to ring your stepfather to let him know you've arrived safely?'

'Yes, please,' said Fathima. 'He'd like that.'

'I'll bring the telephone to your room so you can have some privacy,' said Tanoo.

'This word privacy, what does it mean?' asked Fathima.

'It means so you can be on your own, in private.'

'Ah, I understand.'

'Do you play Cluedo?' asked Venkat who had followed them into the bedroom. 'It's a board game and the murderer is usually Colonel Mustard with the lead piping.'

Fathima looked puzzled. 'Not now, Venkat,' said Tanoo. 'Fathima has had a long journey, she's tired and just wants to unpack, settle in and telephone her family. Would you like a cup of tea, Fathima?'

'Yes, please,' replied Fathima. 'I'll start to unpack and put my things away.'

'Good, I'll bring the telephone and tea to your room. When you've finished unpacking and speaking to your stepfather, just come to the kitchen. So, welcome home.'

'Thank you,' said Fathima.

And so it was that Fathima Mylvaganam arrived at 20 Forest Hill in Baildon.

Chapter 3

John and Liz Campbell also lived on Forest Hill, a winding hilly cul-de-sac with detached properties and cherry trees lining both sides of the road. The trees were not yet in bloom but John always thought that their season was so short and was over almost as soon as it had begun.

The Campbell's house was a 1920s bungalow designed rather like a cricket pavilion with a balcony and an oblong-shaped garden running down to a pond, in which they kept fish. Sun loungers were on the balcony. The boundary of their garden was surrounded by *cupressus leylandii* trees which were kept to a height of six feet by annual trimming, so as not to offend the neighbours, and provided a good deal of privacy. They were about a mile from the centre of Baildon village.

They had lived there for ten years and had a nine-year-old boy, Henry, who went to Bradford Grammar School's Junior School, Clock House. They loved Baildon and its close proximity to Shipley Glen, a moorland area leading to Eldwick, near Bingley to the west. Yet, on a good day, it was only fifteen minutes to Bradford city centre.

Next door to John and Liz lived a chap called Doctor Chaminda Jayasuriya and his wife, Tanoo. John called him Jay for short. John had a typical neighbourly relationship with Jay, talking to him regularly over the hedge when they were working in their back gardens or when they were in their driveways and gardens at the front of their houses.

John and Liz knew that Jay and Tanoo had one child, a ten-year-old boy called Venkat. Jay had come to Leeds University from Newcastle nine months earlier. He commuted every day to the Leeds School of Medicine where John understood he was a lecturer and demonstrator in anatomy.

This was all John and Liz knew about him apart from the fact that he was a keen cricket supporter. He would often talk to John about watching cricket at Galle, which was near his home in Sri Lanka. Galle was one of the world's most beautiful cricket grounds and the site of several memorable test matches between Sri Lanka and England.

John had watched some of those matches on television and longed for the day he could fly to Sri Lanka to watch cricket there. Sadly, it had been flooded and devastated during the tsunami. The fortress-type outline had remained intact and the cricket ground had now been reclaimed. Cricket was the main topic of conversation between John and Jay. Occasionally Jay would talk about politics in Sri Lanka and about the Dalai Lama, the Buddhist religious leader. From that, John assumed Jay was a Buddhist.

John thought Jay to be a very private man, with few friends other than some in the Sri Lankan community in Bradford.

About nine weeks earlier, approximately March 2008, a young Sri Lankan girl arrived at Jay's house. She was in her teens. Tanoo introduced her as their au pair, whom they had hired to look after Venkat whilst Tanoo was at work at the garden centre in nearby Otley. Her name was Fathima, a pleasant but shy girl who spoke good English for her age. John thought, unkindly, that the name fitted. He remembered Fathima Whitbread, a great British shot putter.

In July, John took a week's holiday but stayed at home to save money. Venkat was at home during his school holidays and would come to play cricket with Henry on the lawn at the side of the house. John had bought stumps, a bat and a ball, so that kept them occupied. Fathima would often accompany him.

She seemed a happy girl.

'I love this country,' she said to Liz. 'With green fields and trees everywhere. There's such a variety of countryside. I was very apprehensive at first, I felt extremely homesick and it was so cold and wet the day I arrived but I have settled in now. I went to Ilkley on the bus yesterday with Venkat and we had tea at Betty's. Next week we are going by bus to Harrogate and will go to Betty's there. And the weather is much better now. Back home they say it always rains in England.'

'Don't you believe it,' said Liz. 'We have some lovely summers but we need the rain to keep everything green. By the way, Betty's in Harrogate is very expensive.'

'Where else would you go?' asked Fathima.

'Try Skipton,' replied Liz. 'That's a lovely town. How long do you expect to stay in Baildon?'

'As long as Jay and Tanoo want me. I am improving my English and that will set me in good stead when I go home.'

Liz was left with the distinct impression that Fathima was staying for some time, was very happy living in Baildon and got on well with her charge, Venkat, and his parents.

Fathima would call most days for a chat and a coffee and would help Liz with her housework. Liz enjoyed her company and got the impression the feeling was reciprocated, despite the age difference. Meanwhile, John spoke to Jay almost daily and nothing seemed untoward in the household next door.

Then, one day in late August, when John and Liz were barbecuing in the garden, they heard banging and shouting next door. They had never heard anything like it before but the noise soon died down and peace and quiet prevailed. John was tempted to go round to see if he could help but thought better of it, nor would he mention it to Jay as it really wasn't any of his business.

In September, Fathima suddenly stopped visiting. Liz thought nothing of it for a time, imagining that she was busy and going on more sightseeing trips with Venkat. John, however, also noticed that Jay was seldom to be seen except on the odd occasion when he was gardening. He seemed to be avoiding contact with John who thought: *if that's the way he wants it, there's nowt so queer as folk.*

One day, Liz bumped into Jay as he was going to work. 'Hi Jay,' she said. 'How are things?'

'Fine, I'm very busy at work. I must rush.' And off he went.

That evening, as they cleared away after supper, John and Liz talked about her encounter with Jay.

'It's funny,' said Liz. 'Fathima seems to have just disappeared. She said she loved it in Yorkshire and was improving her English by going to classes in Baildon village hall. She visited regularly and then suddenly she's gone. I wonder what's happened to her?'

'Well,' said John. 'First of all, it's none of our business. We are not a nanny state which spies on our neighbours. There must be some logical explanation. Maybe Jay told her not to bring Venkat around to our house anymore. I don't know. Maybe he thought you were a bad influence. Maybe she has a boyfriend but it's not our business. They are our neighbours for God's sake. We don't want them to think we are being racist if we report her disappearance.'

'I see that,' said Liz. 'I'm sure you're right. We'll not rock the boat, but it is troubling me. I'd love to know where she's gone.'

Chapter 4

Things went on as normal for a couple of weeks. During the third week, John saw Jay in the garden.

'Hi, long time no see. Where've you been hiding?'

'Oh, things have been very busy at the University. We are short staffed and I've had to take on a bigger workload, demonstrating anatomy to medical students,' replied Jay.

'Who's looking after Venkat now?'

'Oh, not Fathima. She had to fly back to Sri Lanka because her mother's ill. Such a shame because she was great. Unfortunately, Tanoo's had to give up her work and she really liked it at the garden centre. We're looking for someone else to look after Venkat. Any ideas?'

'No,' said John. 'But you could put an advert in the local post office. We have got help by doing that in the past.'

'That's a good idea. I'll do that.' Jay then changed the subject. 'What do you think of a man called Nasser Hussain playing for England?'

'He's great and as English as I am. Mind you, my grandfather was an immigrant. Do you plan on staying here?'

'For another couple of years and then we'll go back. I'll look for a job at a University there. I like working as a teacher, it avoids having to deal with patients the whole of the time.'

'I can understand that,' said John. 'Will you be watching Yorkshire on Saturday at Headingley?'

'Maybe, if I've got time. Got to rush. Bye.'

And with that, Jay went back into his house.

That evening, John told Liz about his conversation with Jay.

'She's gone home, her mother's ill.'

'Really, she told me her parents were divorced and she never sees her mother.'

'Maybe, when she became ill, the two were reconciled. Maybe motherly love overcame their differences.'

'Maybe, but I'm still suspicious. Why don't you ask your partner at work?'

Chapter 5

John was a partner in a gardening business on Canal Road in Bradford. His partner, Fred, and he had equal shares in the business and John thought a great deal of him. He was older than John and had recently put on a lot of weight so that he had to wear braces to keep his trousers up.

'You're looking troubled, John. Is there anything I can help you with?' asked Fred.

'Well, as a matter of fact, I'd like your advice on something. The au pair next door, who came from Sri Lanka a few months ago, has disappeared. My neighbour says she's gone back to Sri Lanka because her mother's ill, but my wife has a problem accepting that. I don't, but we agreed I should ask your advice.'

'Well, you could report her as a missing person but the police would simply ask your neighbours whether she is missing and they would say she's gone home. Have you anything more to go on?'

'It's just odd that she never mentioned any problems to my Liz. They used to see each other almost every day and became very friendly, yet she never came to say goodbye. She never left a note. Nothing. We would have invited her for dinner if we'd known she was going. It was all so odd.'

'A difficult one,' said Fred. 'On the one hand, you don't want to seem a troublesome neighbour. Heaven knows, we see plenty of those. On the other hand, if something has happened to her, the iron should be struck while it is still hot. Why not ask around. Did she have any friends of her own age?'

'I don't know of any. I'll make some discreet enquiries. As a last resort, I could report her as missing person but then, if it's a false alarm, neighbourly relations would go down the tube.'

With that, John and Fred got on with their work.

Chapter 6

Liz went shopping as usual on Saturday morning. She enjoyed her walk down into Baildon village to pick up fresh eggs, milk and the newspaper. As she strolled down to the village, she pondered about the history of Baildon and its residents. She had a friend who was a member of the Baildon Local History Society who was always keen to impart her knowledge. Liz also fancied herself as a local historian.

Baildon was famous for being the birthplace of the late Richard Whiteley, who was the front man on the Yorkshire television programme, *Calendar,* and the host of *Countdown* which was the first programme to be aired on Channel 4. It was also the birthplace of the late Ian Clough, one of the best British climbers of his generation, after whom the village hall was named. In 1970, on an expedition to Annapurna, led by Chris Bonnington, Ian was killed on descent by a falling ice-pillar on the mountain's lower slopes.

Liz also knew that other well-known people born in Baildon were Austin Mitchell who also presented *Calendar* with Richard Whiteley and later became the Labour MP for Great Grimsby; former football goalkeeper Bert Hoyle and Coventry City football manager Aidy Boothroyd; and the veteran sports television commentator John Helm who still lives in Baildon.

And among Baildon's famous residents are Brian Close, former Yorkshire and England cricket captain and the young-est man ever to play for England. He played for Yorkshire between 1949 and 1977 and his character and presence made him the most successful county captain of his day. He is now a battle-scarred veteran, hugely popular in Baildon.

Matthew Hoggard also lives in Baildon. He is another excellent cricketer, opening the bowling for England. A strapping pace bowler, capable of swinging the ball both ways. Indeed, as Liz walked into Baildon, Hoggard was playing for England in New Zealand. Liz remembered his hat-trick in Bridgetown, Barbados.

She also remembered the August Bank Holiday weekend when she and John saw over 500 Harley-Davidson riders arrive in Baildon as part of the annual UK rally of the Harley-Davidson Riders Club of Great Britain fundraising rally. The HDRCGB ran the rally up to 2001 when it moved to Berkshire. In 2003, Harley-Davidson's centenary year, the HDRCGB hosted the event for the last time in Baildon. The rally is now organised by the Shipley Harley-Davidson Club and this year, 430 riders were given a police escort down Browgate towards Hollins Hill, from where most riders travelled to Harewood House.

Baildon was an important location for the British gypsy community. A report of 1929 stated that annual gypsy Parties had started two to three hundred years before – records were said to go back to 1770 when it was reported to be an ancient custom. In 1881, up to 5,000 people are said to have paid for admission. Gradually the event was taken over by local residents who dressed up as gypsies and formed 'tribes'. Proceeds went to the local Horticultural Society. After 1897 the tradition died out, apparently because the 'real gypsies' had disappeared. However, in 1929 it was revived to raise funds for Baildon Hospital. A local resident, John Keen, then contacted the so-called 'king of the gypsies', Xavier Petulengro, and they re-established large gypsy gatherings at Baildon, recorded on Pathé News films and shown nationally in cinemas. The gypsy parties ended with the start of the Second World War and were never revived. However, in the early 1990s, travellers used the Bank Holiday loophole to occupy Shipley Glen in Baildon for a weekend festival.

Whilst in the Co-op, built on the site of the old gypsy fairground, she met Fathima's English teacher, Fiona, who was a friend who sang with her in the local choir.

'I'm sorry that Fathima's gone,' said Liz.

'Yes, me too. It's very odd. She just stopped coming for lessons without a word of warning. In fact, she'd paid in advance and never came for a refund. It's most strange.'

'Wasn't it free?' asked Liz.

'No, government cuts and all that. And it would have been a lot of money for her. What's more, she enjoyed the lessons and was doing very well.'

'When she was with me,' said Liz, 'she always spoke very well and she was such a lovely girl. Did she ever say anything to you about leaving?'

'Not a word. What do you know?'

'Well, not a lot. Jay told John her mother was ill and she had to go back to Sri Lanka.'

'Well, she never mentioned that to me,' said Fiona. 'She never even talked about her mother. She mentioned her stepfather a lot, but never her mother. She said her parents were divorced.'

'Has anyone else asked you about her?' said Liz.

'No, except the lollipop lady who controlled the crossing in the village. She asked what had happened to her.'

'Will you ask around? I'll do the same and we'll see if there is anything to worry about.'

'Fine,' said Fiona as they parted company.

* * *

John played cricket for Baildon in the Bradford League. That Saturday afternoon, Phillip Green, one of the young players in his team, came up to him. 'Do you know what's happened to Fathima?' he asked. 'I know she lived next door to you. She told me about you and how the lad she looks after plays cricket with your Henry in your garden.'

'No, I don't know what's happened to her. Why? Did you know her?' asked John.

'Yes, we were going out. I was due to go to the pub with her last Saturday night, but she never showed up. She always complained of being broke and not being paid enough. I miss her. We had a good time together. It's so unlike her just to leave like that without saying a word. I'm really quite upset about it.'

'Well, we can't understand what's happened to her either. If I hear anything, I'll let you know.'

After the game, John told Liz what Phillip had said.

'Well, that fits with what Fiona, her teacher, said to me today in the Co-op. She just stopped going to the class and, what's more, she had paid in advance and she could have got a refund. Anyway, how would she pay for her air fare?'

'Maybe she had an open return ticket but she never mentioned it,' said John.

'Well, I think you should report that she's missing.'

'That will cause real friction with Jay and Tanoo. If they stop allowing Venkat to come round to play, Henry will be very upset.'

'Need they know it is us who have reported it?'

'Maybe not.'

'What's the first step?'

'I'll look up 'missing persons' on the internet.'

They both searched Google which told them to dial 101 or

go to the nearest police station which, for John, was Shipley Police Station on Baildon Green.

'I'll go now,' said John. 'Do you want to come with me?'

'Yes, but we'd better leave it until Monday morning.'

So, the following Monday they went to Shipley Police Station. It was on John's route to work, so they took two cars. They went to the counter and said what they wanted to say to the police officer on duty. They were given a form to complete, which they did, but neither knew Fathima's surname.

When they had finished, John asked if his identity needed to be disclosed.

'Maybe not at first, but if the investigation is followed through, it may be inevitable,' said the officer.

'We understand,' said John and they left.

Chapter 7

On Monday evening, a police constable in uniform arrived at John and Liz's. He parked his Ford Escort police car directly outside.

'God,' said John, 'I hope no one's in next door.'

He told the young policeman all he knew about Fathima having gone missing, as did Liz.

'We'll check the airlines,' he said. 'If she's shown on the passenger list, we'll know it's true that she's gone. We have a bracket of dates so it shouldn't be too difficult.'

'Many thanks,' said John. 'I hope we've done the right thing.'

'Well, you never know. If something has happened to her and you hadn't reported it, you would kick yourselves,' said the police constable.

'That's true,' replied John. 'But I'm sure it's nothing.'

* * *

The following morning, Detective Chief Inspector James Turnbull was at his desk in his office at Bradford police head-quarters. Detective Sergeant Dave Jasper sat at another desk. They had recently concluded the investigation and trial of five men at Teesside Crown Court.

Turnbull was fifty-two. He had been head of the Bradford Murder Squad for several years. He was enjoying the summer as they weren't too busy and, in the evenings, he was able to go to his allotment in Idle where he was growing vegetables. His wife, Sandra, worked part-time in the local medical centre.

Turnbull was also thinking about the weekend he had just enjoyed with Sandra at Bowness-on-Windermere. They had stayed at the Belsfield Hotel where the manager had upgraded them to a suite when he found out he was a policeman. It was a lovely gesture. The rooms had large sash windows overlooking the lake. He and Sandra had been on two boat trips and had taken the open-top bus to Grasmere where they had afternoon tea. *Oh, happy days,* he thought.

Dave was a dapper twenty-nine-year-old bachelor with a love of nice clothes and attractive girls. He loved cars and had an old MGB which was his pride and joy.

The two had worked together for a year. The rest of the team were in an adjacent office.

James was thinking about how Bradford had changed over the years. So much so, he hardly recognised it. From being a wealthy industrial city, famous for its wool and textile trade, to one which seemed down at heel. Bradford's wealthy had left to live in Ilkley, or some such posh place, and many members of the Jewish community, once strong in Bradford, had moved out to Leeds.

His thoughts were disturbed by the ringing of his phone.

'Hi James, it's Raymond here from Missing Persons. How are you? Long time, no see.'

James knew Raymond Little, the inspector in charge of Missing Persons, of old. They had worked together in CID when they were both sergeants. Their biggest case was the Yorkshire Ripper enquiry. Peter Sutcliffe, who became known as the Yorkshire Ripper, lived in Heaton in Bradford.

'I'm well,' replied James. 'Not too busy at the moment. Have you something for me?'

'Well, maybe. An au pair girl from Baildon is said to have gone missing. I say "said to have" purposefully because the family she was staying with suggest she's gone back to Sri Lanka.'

'That's an odd one. What makes you think it's up our street?'

'Well, I've checked the airlines which fly to Sri Lanka and there's no record of her ever flying back. It may be nothing, but my nose tells me there's something fishy about it and I thought you should know.'

'What's her name?'

'We've checked the agencies which provide au pairs and we think we've found her. Her name is Fathima Mylvaganam from Colombo in Sri Lanka.'

'What are the employers called?'

'Chaminda Jayasuriya and Tanoo Jayasuriya of 22 Forest Hill, Baildon. He's a doctor and lecturer in anatomy at Leeds University.'

'Can you e-mail all you know so far and Dave and I will pay them a visit. They sound to be a perfectly respectable family. I assume nothing is known about them, no convictions?'

'No. Clean as a whistle. It's a strange one. Keep me in the loop. How are things otherwise?'

'After the *honour killing* enquiry, I took Sandra to Paris for four days. She loved it but, God, it's expensive.'

'Well, our exchange rate is like that of a third world country these days but that's life. Nice to speak to you. Keep me in the loop.'

They rang off.

Chapter 8

James Turnbull waited for Dave Jasper to return to their office.

'Let's go get a cup of coffee and I'll fill you in on my phone call from Raymond Little,' said Turnbull as Dave walked into the office. They went down to the coffee machine and he told Jasper what Raymond from Missing Persons had told him.

'First of all, I think we need to check the airlines again,' said Jasper. 'We don't want to be going off on a wild goose chase.'

'No, I agree,' said Turnbull. 'Meanwhile, I will speak to the University and find out from his Head of Department what they think of our man.'

Each then went to carry out his task and the two men met again in their office an hour later. Neither had anything to report. Nothing from the airlines and the man from the University spoke very highly of Jayasuriya. He said he was an excellent doctor and demonstrator in anatomy.

'Let's telephone and arrange an appointment to see them. This evening okay with you?'

'Sure.'

'Let's say six o'clock.'

* * *

Turnbull and Jasper arrived at Forest Hill bang on six o'clock. Turnbull liked Baildon. It had a village atmosphere, yet it was within striking distance of Shipley and Bradford.

They were invited in by Tanoo who took them through to their sitting room which was furnished in modern style with prints of Yorkshire scenes adorning the walls. The room was spotless. She introduced them to Jay.

'We're sorry to disturb you,' said Turnbull. 'I'm sure it's nothing, but we've had a report that your au pair girl, Miss Mylvagaman, may be missing. Perhaps you can advise us that she is fit and well.'

'Of course,' said Jay. 'She has gone home to Sri Lanka.'

'Can you tell me when she went?'

'I'm not sure. Maybe six weeks ago. Is that right, Tanoo?'

'Yes,' she said. 'About six weeks ago.'

'Did she fly direct?'

'I assume so.'

'Did you take her to the airport and, if so, which one?'

'I think she was intending to fly from Leeds Bradford to London and then on to Sri Lanka.'

'Did you buy her a ticket?'

'No, her stepfather had bought her an open return.'

'How did she get to the airport?'

'I assume by taxi.'

'Didn't you see her off?'

'No. I said goodbye to her and then went to work.'

'Did she have luggage?'

'Yes.'

'Did she have any money?'

'I gave her a hundred pounds.'

'Did you see her tickets?'

'No.'

'So, you don't know which airline she flew with?'

'I assume Emirates.'

'Have you a photo of her?'

'No.'

'You mean to tell me you never took any photographs of her with your child?'

'No, we never did.'

'How did she come here?'

'Through an agency.'

'Did she go suddenly?'

'Yes, she said her mother had been taken ill.'

'So, there was no disagreement?'

'No, it was her mother's illness that caused her to leave.'

'Do you know her mother's name?'

'No.'

'Do you know Fathima's date of birth?'

'No.'

'Did she say goodbye to friends?'

'I don't know.'

'Don't you have any documentation from the agency giving her details?'

'No.'

'Why not?'

'Well, I had some originally but, when she went, I threw them away.'

'Didn't it occur to either of you to make a note of her birthday? It must have been on the form and I would have thought that if you employ someone and they are actually living with you, you would want to be able to celebrate their birthday one way or another.'

'No, I didn't make a note of it.'

'Well, Dr Jayasuriya, we cannot find any trace of her flying to Sri Lanka.'

'That's extraordinary. Maybe she flew somewhere en route to Sri Lanka, or maybe she flew on someone else's ticket.'

'Whose could that be?'

'I don't know. She had a lot of Sri Lankan friends. I discouraged that because I thought she should have English friends so that she could get used to the way of life here and speak more English.'

'Can we look at her room?'

'Yes, of course.'

Turnbull and Jasper were shown into a pretty bedroom with a view on to the garden and beyond it to Shipley Glen.

'Do you mind leaving us?' asked Turnbull.

'No. We'll be in the sitting room,' said Jay as he left the room.

'Dave, look for anything she may have left here,' said Turnbull.

They searched for half an hour but didn't find anything. Then, suddenly, Jasper said, 'Bingo'. He had found two hundred pounds in twenty pound notes under the mattress.

They looked in the adjoining bathroom where they found a toothbrush but nothing else, and then returned to the sitting room.

'Dr Jayasuriya, can you explain the two hundred pounds we've found under her mattress?'

'Maybe it's not hers. It could have been left there by mistake by our last visitors from Sri Lanka.'

'Has anyone reported it missing?'

'No.'

'Well, thank you, Dr Jayasuriya. You've been most helpful. We'll be in touch.'

Jasper drove them back to headquarters.

'What did you think?' asked Turnbull.

'I don't believe him that the money could have been left by someone else. I am sure that money was hers and, if it was, there's no way she would leave it behind; particularly if she wasn't intending to return.'

'I agree. Let's get the team together and have a meeting on Monday morning at ten o'clock.'

Chapter 9

At ten o'clock on the Monday morning, Turnbull's team met in the boardroom at Bradford headquarters. Present were Turnbull, Jasper, Detective Sergeant John Roberts and Detective Constable Jane Rowley. Jane dispensed coffee from the machine on the side table, a job to which she silently objected as she thought it sexist.

'Morning all,' said Turnbull.

'We have a possible missing au pair on our hands. We don't know yet where she's gone or what's happened to her, but the circumstances are such that Inspector Raymond Little, from Missing Persons, has a feeling that something's not right. I trust his instinct; he has a nose for this sort of thing, so much so that I feel justified in making some preliminary enquiries.

'The girl is called Fathima Mylvaganam from Colombo, Sri Lanka. She is in her late teens and is, or was, employed by Doctor Chaminda Jayasuriya and his wife, Tanoo, as an au pair for their son, Venkat. They live at 22 Forest Hill, Baildon.

'Fathima was last seen six weeks or so ago by the next-door neighbours, John and Liz Campbell, who live at number twenty.

'The Jayasuriyas say that the girl has gone back to Sri Lanka on an open ticket. Dave has checked with all the airlines and there's no trace of her on any passenger list.

'It seems she left suddenly, not telling anyone other than the Jayasuriyas. They said she told them that her mother was ill. When we searched her bedroom, we found two hundred pounds in twenty pound notes under her mattress, which seems very odd. When we told the Jayasuriyas about it, they said that it could have been left there by one of their visitors from Sri Lanka, but I don't buy that.

'Her English teacher in Baildon, to whom she was quite close, was not told that her mother was ill, neither was her boyfriend, Phillip Green, whom she stood up. Neither knew she was leaving the UK.

'I think we should extend our enquiries to people she associated with. Dave, can you make enquiries at the Buddhist temples in Bradford and Leeds. There are three in Leeds according to my researches. Each has a bikkhu or monk in charge. She may have attended one or more of them.'

'Yes, will do.'

'John, you take cafés and restaurants frequented by the Sri Lankan community in Bradford, Leeds and surrounding areas. Also, any pubs that are frequented by Sri Lankans.'

'Will do. Is it okay if I take Nuwan with me? He's a traffic cop. He's from Sri Lanka originally and speaks the language, whatever that is.'

'Yes, that's a good idea. Jane, you check whether there is a club for Sri Lankans in Bradford, Leeds and surrounding areas. Also, can you search on Facebook to see whether there is a local Sri Lankan Society listed, or if Fathima is on Facebook, and will you ring the police in Sri Lanka? The official language there is Sinhala, but it's also listed as English so you shouldn't have a problem. If you do, get Nuwan to help you.'

'Yes, I'll get on to it right away.'

'Thanks everyone. I will speak to her boyfriend and also check the whereabouts of the Dalai Lama. If he, as the spiritual leader of the Buddhists, has come to Europe, she may have gone on a pilgrimage. I'll also check the airlines to see if she could have slipped through the net that way.

'I suggest we meet here again in two or three days' time. As you've all got quite a bit to get through, let's say Thursday at ten o'clock. Any questions? No, well let's go.'

Chapter 10

Dave Jasper went home after the team meeting. He lived alone in a cottage in the village of Rawdon, just outside Bradford, on the Harrogate Road. It was a good area, as a result of which it stretched his finances to buy it, but it was well worth it.

He had lived in Rawdon for most of his life, having been educated at Woodhouse Grove School – a private school – and then on to Bradford University to read geography. His father had been an accountant in Bradford and was now retired.

Dave was thirty and had just passed his Inspectors' exams, but because of cuts and congestion on the promotion ladder, he still had the rank of Detective Sergeant. However, he enjoyed being in the Murder Squad under DCI James Turnbull. He learnt a lot from him and was slowly controlling his impatience which he knew to be a failing.

He was a bachelor but loved the company of girls even though his hours meant hanging on to a lasting relationship was difficult. He was a snappy dresser and liked his image. His car was an MGB GT which he had recently bought at a classic car auction.

He poured himself a gin and slimline tonic and put on a CD of Frank Sinatra, his favourite singer, before heading upstairs to shower and change into his jeans and a sweater. When he returned to his sitting room, he picked up the latest P D James novel he was reading and settled into his favourite chair.

He wanted to model himself on Police Commander Adam Dalgleish, her famous detective. Dalgleish was controlled; he had authority but never raised his voice. He had a bright mind and was a well-read poet. He was a bachelor like Dave and was discreet. Dave eventually fell asleep reading about him, it had been a tiring day. He woke up at 3:00 a.m. and went upstairs to bed.

The following morning, he was up at 7:00 a.m. and had muesli and toast for breakfast. Nothing too fattening as he had a good physique, was in good shape for a man of six feet two, and he wanted to stay that way.

After breakfast, before setting off for the Jamyang Buddhist Centre in Leeds, he spent the morning at home. He checked the previous day's post, caught up with some paperwork and his notebook entries. It was much easier to get to Leeds from his home and Turnbull had agreed he needn't report to HQ until later. He aimed to arrive at the Buddhist centre about lunchtime for the nondenominational meditation session.

He received a warm and friendly welcome at the Buddhist centre. The place was a haven of peace, an oasis of tranquillity in a busy area of Leeds. Dave spotted a monk who looked Sri Lankan and appeared to be in charge. He approached him and explained the reason for his visit.

The bikkhu, which apparently was his official title, invited Dave into his office.

'I gather you aren't here to meditate. Pity, it would help your wellbeing. Please come back another time and we can chat about that. You asked about a girl called Fathima Mylvaganam. Yes, by chance, I do know her. You are lucky to find me because there are lots of Buddhist centres in West Yorkshire – there's one in Shipley, Halifax, Keighley and Bradford – but we pride ourselves on being the most popular centre. Fathima also went to meditation classes in Bradford.'

'We are concerned about her,' said Dave. 'She seems to have disappeared and we fear something may have happened to her.'

'How dreadful,' said the bikkhu. 'She was last here about six weeks ago and I have often wondered why she stopped coming. I just assumed she was going to one of the centres nearer her home. Please tell me what you know.'

'Well, not a lot really. She was working as an au pair and suddenly disappeared. Dr Jayasuriya, for whom she worked, says she has gone back to Sri Lanka because her mother is ill. Did she mention this to you?'

'No, not a word. Nor did she mention it in classes. She loved it here and was very fond of the young boy she was looking after. I think he was called Venkat.'

'Did she ever complain about her employers?'

'No, quite the contrary. She liked the doctor and his wife very much. I understand they are also Buddhists, but they don't come here.'

'So, you have no idea why she should suddenly leave?'

'No, none at all. Indeed, she enrolled for classes and then suddenly stopped coming without an explanation.'

'Well, many thanks for your time,' said Dave. 'I'll let you know if we find her.'

'Thank you. I would appreciate that.'

Dave went back to his car and to the hustle and bustle of Leeds city centre.

Chapter 11

John Roberts was also a Detective Sergeant in the Bradford Murder Squad. He was forty-five and had no ambition to go any further. He had come up through the ranks, not like pretty boy Dave Jasper. John was married with two children who were still at school, locally, in Eccleshill.

John's task was to go to the cafés and restaurants frequented by the Sri Lankan community to see if anyone knew Fathima Mylvaganam.

As arranged, he collected Nuwan on Manningham Lane. Nuwan was Sri Lankan and served in the Bradford police force as a traffic cop.

'Hi, Nuwan,' said John. 'Where do you suggest we start?'

'I suggest we go to the Tharavadu Café in the centre of Leeds. That's as good a place as any to start cos it's a favourite meeting place for young Sri Lankans to hang out. I know the owner.'

They arrived there in time for coffee. The café had tables outside on the pavement and the Sri Lankan flag hung over the entrance. Inside, the television was on and several men were glued to a Sri Lankan cricket match.

Nuwan spoke to the owner and introduced him to John.

'Nice to meet you. Coffee?'

'Yes please, white no sugar,' replied John.

'Same for me please,' said Nuwan.

'Take a seat and I'll bring it over.'

The three of them sat at one of the tables in a quiet corner of the restaurant.

'As Nuwan has explained,' said John. 'We are trying to

ascertain the whereabouts of a Sri Lankan girl called Fathima Mylvaganam and wondered if she might have been a customer here?'

'Yes, I know Fathima. She came here with an English boyfriend called Phillip. She came almost every week on her evenings off. She was always very chatty, but suddenly she stopped coming.'

'Did she ever tell you that she was leaving?' asked John.

'No. In fact, the last time she was here, she told me they would be coming again the following week. She booked a table but never turned up.'

'Did she ever talk about her mother?'

'No, she used to talk about her stepfather who had given his blessing for her to come to the UK, but never about her mother.'

'Do you know if she went to any other haunts frequented by Sri Lankans?'

Nuwan translated when a puzzled look crossed the café owner's face.

'No, this is the place they came to as far as I am aware. She may have been on the website all the young ones are on. What's it called? Oh, yes, Facebook. Try that.'

'Thanks,' said John. 'We'll do that.'

They watched the cricket for a few minutes as they finished their coffee.

'Got to be off,' said Nuwan. 'Thanks.'

* * *

Jane Rowley's task was to check out the Sri Lankan clubs in the area and to go on Facebook. Jane was the computer expert in the squad. She also had to ring the Sri Lankan police. She thought she could do her job from her desk in the squad room without having to go out in the rain. She was not feeling on good form as it was the wrong time of the month.

Jane had always promised herself that she would not date a policeman after an incident in Sheffield which she wanted to forget. But, last night, she had met a Detective Sergeant in Leeds where they were both attending the thirtieth birthday party of a mutual friend.

She had agreed to go for a drink with him after the party. It was a mistake from the word go and when he started pawing her, she told him to bugger off and got a taxi home. Oh, for a man who thought of more than one thing.

Back to work.

She found Fathima on Facebook fairly quickly. Her last entry had been in April. "I am writing this in English for practise," she wrote. "I've been with Venkat on Shipley Glen. There is a small train there which Venkat loves. I am going out with Phillip tonight to the Tharavadu at 8:00 p.m. if anyone wants to come. I like Phillip, but he spends too much time playing cricket! I suppose it doesn't matter much cos I have little free time. Just bought some new shoes in the sale at Stead and Simpsons. Picture attached. Everything fine for me."

Jane was excited. She now had an up-to-date picture of Fathima smiling as she showed off her new shoes. No mention on Facebook of her mother being ill or of leaving the UK.

Next, Jane went on Google to find the addresses and telephone numbers of local Sri Lankan societies. She found one in Bradford and called them. After introducing herself, she asked to speak to the secretary.

'I am the secretary. How can I help you?'

Jane explained who she was and said, 'We're trying to trace a girl called Fathima Mylvaganam. Do you know her?'

'Yes, she is a member of our Society.'

'What do you know about her?'

'We hold meetings at the Polish Club on Manningham Lane in Bradford. She came to the meetings from time-to-time.'

'When did you last see her?'

'She stopped coming some months ago.'

'Did she say why?'

'No.'

'Did she ever say she was returning to Sri Lanka cos her mother was ill?'

'Not so far as I know.'

'Anything else you can tell me?'

She once brought an English boy called Phillip but he soon got bored because everyone spoke in our language.'

'Thank you for your help. Goodbye.'

'That's okay. Bye.'

Well, it now looks as though she just disappeared, thought Jane. *Now for the difficult bit, ringing Sri Lanka.* She spent nearly an hour making several phone calls.

When Jane mentioned the name Fathima Mylvaganam, she could sense that she'd hit a nerve.

'Who did you say?' asked the Sri Lankan officer.

'Fathima Mylvaganam,' she replied.

'I'll call you back,' he said.

More time wasted, Jane thought. However, five minutes later her telephone rang.

'I'm calling from Sri Lankan police headquarters. I'm the Inspector General of Police, Sri Lanka's most senior police officer, equivalent to your commissioner. I'm directly answerable to the Minister for Home Affairs.'

'Yes, sir,'. said Jane, sitting up and wondering what pot she had stirred to get someone as important as the Inspector

General involved.

'Do you know who this girl is?' he asked.

'No, only her name,'

'Then let me tell you. She is the daughter of our Minister for Home Affairs, Angelo Mylvaganam. He's the equivalent of your Home Secretary.'

'Oh, my God,' said Jane. 'We'd no idea. At present we're treating this as a missing persons enquiry.'

'Well, the Sri Lankan government is in sensitive talks with the Indian government at the moment,' said the commissioner. 'I can't go into any details, but maybe it's just a coincidence. Perhaps she's been kidnapped by some extremists who want to gain some political advantage.

'The Sri Lankan relations with India have deteriorated in the 1980s with the rise of Tamil militant separatism. Sri Lanka is only thirty nautical miles from India and, historically, relations with India have been fraught with controversies, particularly over fishing rights.'

'I understand,' said Jane. 'Please can you make enquiries at your end to be sure she hasn't somehow flown back to Sri Lanka?'

'Of course, we'll do that. We'll have to inform the Minister that his daughter has disappeared. He will be distraught.'

'Can I leave that up to you as it would be better if he could be told in person rather than on the telephone?'

'Of course. I'll go and see him straight away. He may want us to send a Sri Lankan officer to work with you and he may want to come over himself.'

'Well,' said Jane. 'I assure you that the officer in charge is highly competent.'

'Very well, we'll hold back on that for the moment. Please will you ring me daily to keep me informed?'

Jane agreed and took down the number. The call ended. *Interesting,* she thought, *the boss won't like this.*

Jane spoke to Turnbull as a matter of urgency and told him the startling news. No sooner had she told him, his internal line rang. It was the Chief Constable.

'Turnbull, I've just had a call from the Home Secretary. He's had a call from his opposite number in Sri Lanka, the Minister for Home Affairs. I suppose you know by now that the girl who's gone missing is his bloody daughter or, apparently, adopted daughter.

'We were not informed of her arrival in the UK, otherwise we'd have kept an eye on her. What's the situation?'

'Well, sir, she was reported missing by the next door neighbours. We've made the usual enquiries in the neighbourhood after Missing Persons reported it to us. So far, we've no positive information. I'm due to interview the family this evening.'

'Well, the Sri Lankans are really twitchy. They fear there may be political undertones. Please keep me informed, a daily update would be appreciated.'

'No problem. I'll keep in touch,' said Turnbull.

* * *

Angelo Mylvaganam was very twitchy. Indeed, much more than that. He was overcome with grief. He regarded Fathima as his own daughter. He had, in effect, adopted her when she was eight years old and he had a loving, fatherly relationship with her. He had allowed her to go the UK. *How stupid,* he thought.

The Inspector General of Police had rung him to inform him that his daughter had gone missing in the UK. Angelo had told him that he hoped this was not political and related to their talks with the Indian government. The Inspector General had said he doubted it but, nevertheless, Angelo had asked him to make thorough enquiries to ascertain whether or not she could have returned to Sri Lanka.

Angelo found it very difficult to believe that she would return to Sri Lanka without contacting her friends or coming home to him.

The Inspector General mounted a nationwide search for Fathima. Two days later, he rang Angelo. 'No joy, I'm afraid. No sign of her having returned to Sri Lanka.'

'Tell me when the trial is. I'll go over. And please tell your contact in the UK to tell the police that I deposited two thousand pounds in an account for Fathima at Barclays Bank in Baildon.

'Yes,' said the Inspector General. 'I'll do that now. I'll ring the UK.'

* * *

James Turnbull got Phillip Green's details from Dr Jay's next-door-neighbour, John Campbell. He rang him on his landline but there was no reply so he tried his mobile. Still no reply, so he left a message. Shortly thereafter, his phone rang.

'Hi, it's Phillip Green, Fathima's friend. How can I help?'

'Well,' said Turnbull. 'As I said in my message, I am a police officer and I want to talk to you about Fathima who has been reported as a missing person. We are trying to establish where she is. What can you tell me about her and when did you last see her?'

'Okay,' said Phillip. 'We were going out. I met her in a pub in Baildon. She was with other Sri Lankan girls. We got chatting and I asked her out. We went out a few times. She took me to a Sri Lankan restaurant in Leeds and once to a

Sri Lankan Society meeting. We were getting on really well. I have a car and I'd pick her up from the house in Baildon where she worked and lived.

'Then she just stood me up. I went to collect her one night and her boss said she wasn't there and he closed the door in my face. I assumed she had just changed her mind, but it was odd that she never rang me. It wasn't like her.'

'And you never saw her again?' asked Turnbull.

'No.'

'How did she seem in herself?'

'Very happy. She talked a lot about home, but that's only natural. I agree. I think she's gone missing.'

'Did she ever say she had to go back to Sri Lanka cos her mother was ill?'

'No.'

'Many thanks. We'll be in touch to take a statement from you.'

Turnbull then rang the Tibetan Embassy in London. The Dalai Lama had been in Tibet for the last six months.

* * *

At ten o'clock on the Thursday, the same group met again in the boardroom, so called because of the large oblong mahogany table surrounded by a dozen chairs. The walls were adorned with photographs of Chief Constables. DCI Turnbull addressed the meeting.

'You probably all know by now that our missing person is an important person in that she's the daughter of the Home Affairs Minister in Sri Lanka, so our Home Secretary is following our progress.

'Dave, what have you got?' asked Turnbull.

'Well, I've checked all three Buddhist temples and found that Fathima attended one in Harehills, Leeds, from time to time. I spoke to the bikkhu who knows her. She attended about six weeks ago and said nothing to him about her mother being ill or about leaving the UK. He got the impression that she was very happy here.

'I also found a Buddhist centre in Halifax and a couple of places in Bradford and Keighley where meditation classes are held, but there wasn't anyone at any of these places who knew Fathima.'

'What's your feeling? What do your antennae tell you?'

'I think it's possible she's been murdered or kidnapped. Something's very odd.'

'Thanks Dave. John, have you got anything to report?'

'Yes, Nuwan and I found that the Leeds Sri Lankan community frequent a café called the Tharavadu in LS1 5DQ. We paid them a visit and spoke to the owner who knows her. He told us she had been there a lot with her English boyfriend and was always very chatty with the staff. She didn't say anything to any of them about leaving or about her mother being ill in Sri Lanka.'

'What's your feel for the case?'

'I agree with Dave. Something odd's happened here.'

'Thanks John. Jane, anything?'

'Yes, I found that there's a Sri Lankan Society in Bradford, they meet at the Polish Club on Manningham Lane. Fathima had been a few times but stopped going a while ago. Fathima did use Facebook but never posted anything online about leaving the UK or her mother being ill. She spoke about how happy she was to be in England and I have a recent photograph of her showing off some new shoes she'd bought.

'I rang the Sri Lankan police, as you suggested. It took some time to get through to someone who knew anything, but when I said we were investigating the possible murder of a young Sri Lankan au pair girl called Fathima Mylvaganam I could sense that they were beginning to twitch.

'Apparently, this type of work is very much encouraged in Sri Lanka and there's been a lot of positive press about the subject.

'Their Inspector General of Police rang me back after making enquiries. Firstly, they found that Fathima was engaged through a respectable agency. What is interesting is that Jayasuriya requested this girl by name. The agency got in touch with her and she and her stepfather agreed that she could come to the UK. Her parents were divorced and she was brought up by her stepfather who is the Minister for Home Affairs in Sri Lanka.

'I am awaiting a copy of her birth certificate which should come through by e-mail this morning.'

'What's your feel?'

'I agree with the other two. Something odd has happened. The Sri Lankan police are very concerned. They've made a thorough search for her in Sri Lanka and there's no sign of her. Also, her stepfather deposited two thousand pounds in an account in her name at Barclays Bank, Baildon.'

'Good work. Thanks Jane. Let me know when you get the birth certificate.' Said Turnbull. 'Well, I've spoken to the boyfriend, Phillip Green, who told me he went with her to the restaurant which has been referred to and to a Sri Lankan Society meeting. She never mentioned about her mother being ill or about leaving. Her behaviour in just standing him up is totally out of character.

'I've also checked on the Dalai Lama's whereabouts. He is, and has been for the last six months, in Tibet. So a pilgrimage is not an explanation.'

'Has anyone any more ideas?' asked Turnbull. 'Are we justified now in seeking a search warrant?'

Everyone nodded in agreement.

'Very well, tomorrow I'll go before the Bradford Magistrates to apply for a search warrant and an order of disclosure of her bank details. We'll meet again at two o'clock tomorrow afternoon.'

Just as the meeting was breaking up, a woman PC, in uniform, knocked and entered the room. She walked over to Jane. 'Ma'am, I have the e-mail you were expecting.'

Jane looked at the copy of the birth certificate and was visibly shocked. The person named as the father was Chaminda Jayasuriya. She handed it to DCI Turnbull who read it out.

'Well, well, well. Fancy that, Jayasuriya being the girl's father,' said Jasper when they'd returned to their office.

'That puts a different light on everything,' said Turnbull. 'It provides a motive as much as anything else.'

'She could have found out he was her father and they could have argued about it,' said Jasper. 'It's odd that he didn't tell us this, nor did his wife. But there again, maybe she doesn't know. Maybe that day John Campbell heard the shouting and banging, it was Jayasuriya killing her.'

'Don't let's get ahead of ourselves, one step at a time,' said Turnbull. 'Let's get on with the search first. We mustn't jump the gun. Tell the others, will you please? How do you suggest we conduct this search, Dave?'

'Well, we know there's no visible sign of the body in the house. If it's there, it's out of sight, so that means taking the place apart.'

'I agree,' said Turnbull. 'We'll have to ask the Jayasuriyas to move out whilst the search takes place. We'll need a big team if we're to do the job properly. Far more than we have at present. I'll approach Bob Illingworth.'

Bob was the Superintendent in overall charge of the Murder Squad although rarely, if ever, involved in an investigation.

'Bob will probably ask the Chief Constable for support,' said Turnbull. 'I'll ring him now.'

Turnbull explained to Bob Illingworth the state of their enquiry; that the whole team was concerned for the girl's welfare and that he believed a search of the house was now the next step.

Illingworth agreed to approach the Chief Constable.

By the end of the day, thirty men with the appropriate equipment had been identified and they were asked to report to Bradford Headquarters at noon the following day.

James Turnbull was thankful for an early day. It was sunny for a change, with a few wispy clouds passing overhead. He was pleased that Yorkshire, who were playing at Headingley, wouldn't have been rained off.

He got to his home in Idle, Bradford, in time to enjoy the sun in his garden. He sat in his deckchair and admired the view. His house was on a hill and his garden overlooked Shipley to the west with its mill chimneys. He could see Salts Mill with its huge chimney, almost as big as the Lister's Mill chimney which dominated the Bradford skyline and which, it was rumoured, was wide enough at the top for a horse and cart to be driven round.

Salts Mill has become a heritage site in recent years and housed many David Hockney originals which the owners had bought when they were young. It's currently home to the largest collection of Hockneys in the world.

His thoughts returned to the investigation: *If a body was recovered, surely that would establish murder against Jay or possibly his wife. Yet it seemed strange that a highly thought of doctor could act in such a barbaric way. Maybe she just died. No. Surely if that had happened, he would have contacted her family, her doctor or the police. All very strange.* James lit his pipe which he was trying, unsuccessfully, to give up.

Chapter 12

The following morning at ten o'clock, Turnbull went before the Chairman of the Bradford Magistrates and made his application for a search warrant of 22 Forest Hill, Baildon, and an order of disclosure relating to Fathima's bank account. The hearing was held in camera so that the Jayasuriyas would not be tipped off as to what was going to happen. The applications were granted.

Turnbull rang the bank and was informed that the £2,000 remained untouched.

He then returned to headquarters where the search team had begun to assemble. He addressed them on the steps of the police station.

'We're looking for the body of a young girl who disappeared some months ago. Try not to be squeamish. This job has to be done. Sergeant Jones will lead and he will put you in teams and designate an area to each team which must be searched thoroughly. Today we search the garden and exterior of the premises. Nothing can be left to chance. Bill Thornton from SOCO will also be present to supervise.

'I'll go first and serve the search warrant on the occupiers, assuming at least one of them will be at home. You will all then follow fifteen minutes after me. Any questions?'

There were none so Turnbull and Jasper set off for Baildon

* * *

They arrived at 22 Forest Hill at 12:32 p.m. Mrs Jayasuriya was at home.

'Mrs Jayasuriya, we have a warrant to search your house. I suggest you telephone your husband and make arrangements to move out of your home because, I am sorry to say, the search will cause a major disruption.'

Tanoo began crying. 'Why? What have we done wrong?'

'We believe the body of Fathima Mylvaganam may be here,' said Turnbull.

'Oh, my God,' sobbed Tanoo. 'That's not possible. Where shall we go?'

'We have arranged accommodation nearby at the Marriott Hotel on Hollins Hill, which will be paid for. We will make as little disruption as possible and engineers will come after the search to put everything back in place.' Turnbull wasn't hopeful that this would actually happen but he'd try his best.

'I will ring Jay. Can you wait until I've done that?'

'Of course,' said Turnbull. 'Take your time. I'm sure nothing will come of it, but we have to check. You may want to pack a few things for the three of you.'

Tanoo rang her husband on their landline. By chance, Jay answered the phone in his office at Leeds University. Turnbull could sense the shock that the message caused on the other end of the line. She rang off.

'If you gather some things together, we'll run you up to the hotel,' said Turnbull. 'Everything we do will be videoed. You can stay if you wish to watch what we do, or you may leave.'

'I'll go,' she replied. 'But what about my son? Venkat is at school. Can I ring my friend and ask her to pick him up and bring him to the hotel? I'll say we're going there for tea.'

'Yes, that's fine,' said Turnbull. 'Can you do that now and then you can get on your way once you've packed a few things?'

Tanoo made a quick phone call, obviously trying not to

sound upset, and arranged to meet her friend at the hotel with Venkat.'

'I suggest you engage a solicitor, Mrs Jayasuriya,' said Turnbull. 'Do you know one?'

'Not off hand.'

'Well, we've got a list of solicitors experienced in this field,' said Turnbull as Jasper handed her the list. 'You can, if it suits, have the Duty Solicitor.'

'That suits me fine,' she replied.

'Thanks,' said Jasper. 'We'll sort that out for you.'

The team started to arrive and waited outside for the go ahead. Half an hour later, Tanoo entered the living room.

'My suitcases are in the bedroom,' she said.

'We'll fetch them and Sergeant Jasper will take you to the hotel,' said Turnbull.

Ten minutes later, Turnbull addressed the team outside. 'Okay, we're just about ready to go. Report any findings to me. I will be in the house. Bill Thornton from SOCO will be in overall charge.

'You will start with the area outside the house. Work in teams of ten. Dig in a line then move to a line next but one and so on. If you find anything of interest, raise the red flag which I will give to each team. That keeps noise to a minimum.

'I suggest Sergeant Jones identifies an area for each team. No prizes for the first red flag. There may be none. Treat plants and shrubs with care. We hope to have them replanted and the lawn re-laid.'

God, thought Turnbull, *this pleasant garden with flowering shrubs will end up like a ploughed field. Goodness knows what the bill will be for a contract gardener to restore it if we find nothing.*

'Bill Thornton will now address you,' said Turnbull.

'Thank you,' said Bill. 'You all have shovels which are very strong and blunt instruments, capable of a lot of damage. So, when you dig, do it as gently as you possibly can.

'I have a team of sifters here with mesh sieves, trowels and brushes. So, when you think you've found something of relevance, raise your flag and my team will move in. They will then trowel and tease away the earth from around whatever it is and then they'll sift.

'The soil around the object may be discoloured and there may be a smell if muscle fibre or soft tissue is still attached to joints. There may be clothes or hair, so keep a close watch. We've got torches if you need them. For obvious reasons, make sure your shovel is clean before you start. Clean as you can please.

'You may find signs of infestation. Don't kill any beetles or maggots or destroy puparial casings they may have left behind because they are useful to an entomologist to establish the time of death.

'That's all I need to say at present. Good luck.'

The digging began in formation, as instructed.

Bill Thornton came over to speak to James Turnbull. 'Morning, James, haven't seen you since the *honour killing* case. How are you?'

'Very well, thanks, Bill. Not too busy at the moment and enjoying life. How about you?'

'SOCOs are always run off their feet. I'm expecting the pathologist to arrive any minute.'

Almost before the words were out of his mouth, Professor John Talbot arrived. Turnbull greeted him. 'How are things?'

'Well, there's no murder season so dead bodies keep coming. What do you expect to find here?'

'It's possible that the body of a Sri Lankan girl, in her teens, is buried here. If that proves to be the case, you'll have your work cut out matching the skeleton with what is known about the missing girl.'

'Well, I'll get the lab ready to receive whatever is found. My practise is to reconstruct the body, look for signs of violence, et cetera. We may bring in an expert entomologist to say how long the body has been buried. He can usually make an educated guess from the degree of infestation.'

'Well, let's not jump the gun, and think about my budget,' said Turnbull. 'John, do you want to go back to your office and we'll call you if anything transpires? Bill will make sure everything is labelled properly as to where everything is found. It's up to you whether you come back.'

Turnbull knew Professor Talbot of old. He was a highly respected forensic pathologist with his own department which he started at Leeds University.

'I'll go,' said the professor. 'Ring me if there are any developments.'

Turnbull sat in the kitchen of the house bringing his note-book up-to-date. He then tuned the radio in to *Radio LW 198* and listened to the cricket commentary. He didn't know what to expect from the search. In many ways, he hoped it would be a wild goose chase, but somehow his nose told him they'd find something.

Chapter 13

After two hours or so, a PC wearing clothing for the search, knocked on the back door before opening it and informing Turnbull that a red flag had been raised in the area behind the garage.

Turnbull and Bill Thornton walked calmly to the spot where Turnbull looked into the hole dug by the line of men. There, a team of SOCO specialists were trowelling and sifting material from a hole about two feet deep in which there lay a large number of bones, big and small. Turnbull wasn't expert enough to know what they were although they looked like they could be human bones, but there was no hair or signs of clothing. Bill gave directions as to their collection.

Turnbull said to the others who had gathered around, 'Back to work lads.'

During the remainder of the day, the rest of the outside area was dug but nothing else was found that was of any relevance. One PC found an old coin which he asked if he could keep.

'Certainly not,' said Turnbull. 'It belongs to the householder.'

At 5:00 p.m., Turnbull called a halt to the search and asked the team to reconvene in the morning to search the house. They looked exhausted. Jane had brought them all sandwiches and tea at one o'clock and they'd been given a half hour break, but it had been a long day for them. She doubted whether any of them had dug for a whole day before.

'Dave,' Turnbull said to Jasper who had returned from the hotel, 'go to the University and seal off any areas where Jayasuriya worked with human parts.'

'Will do,' said Jasper. 'See you here tomorrow. When do

you want his work-area searched?'

'Tomorrow, after we've finished with the house,' said Turnbull. 'Good work lads. No more digging, you'll be pleased to hear.'

* * *

The following morning, the teams reassembled and each team was given a room to search. Noise reverberated throughout the house as floorboards were lifted.

The team working in the hallway came up with a result very quickly. From three plant pots, bones were recovered which looked, to Turnbull, very much like backbones. Next, from a container in the kitchen, small bones were recovered. These looked like finger bones.

From a holdall in the loft, large bones were recovered. Turnbull thought that these looked like femurs, tibias and fibulas from legs. These items were immediately taken to Professor Talbot's laboratory. Nothing else was recovered from the house despite all the floorboards being pulled up.

What a mess, thought Turnbull. *Maybe we'll learn from this. Don't disturb the fabric unless it's totally necessary.*

Turnbull then went with SOCO Bill Thornton to Leeds University where, from a biology laboratory, a coffee jar was found to contain what looked like human bones. From a steel tray, they recovered what looked like the radius and ulna bones from the arms, also parts of the skull and hip bones. Finally, from a desk drawer in Jay's office, parts of a skull were found.

All the bones recovered were shipped over to Professor Talbot's laboratory where a team was waiting to piece together the bones that had been collected.

It took the team twelve hours of laborious work, after which a whole human skeleton was put together with only a few missing bones and no bones were there which didn't relate to the one body.

Turnbull went to see Professor Talbot in his office.

'Well, James, we have the skeleton of a post-pubertal young girl who was five feet six inches in height. It's difficult to gauge the weight. I can tell she was post-pubertal by the pelvic notch.'

'The bones have been in situ for months. It's difficult to be exact.'

'All that fits,' said Turnbull. 'It's got to be the skeleton of our missing au pair. Is there any way of knowing how she died?'

'Well, there's no impact damage to any of the bones in the skull, arms, legs or chest that I can see. If stabbed, a knife normally causes a nick in the chest bone, but we didn't find that here. She could have been stabbed with the knife not hitting any bone. That's unlikely, but distinctly possible.

'There's one very odd feature. Can you see it, James?'

'No,' replied Turnbull. 'Enlighten me.'

'There are no teeth. All the teeth have been removed and are missing. We can often trace a body by the dental work but, in this case, we can't. This suggests that the teeth have been removed deliberately.

'There are too many things missing to be able to say for certain whose body this is. If we had the skeleton's dental history and teeth had been recovered, we could learn a lot. Whether the person was a smoker or negligent brusher. We could see fillings, any untreated cavities, tartar build up and whether or not he or she had seen a dentist recently. But here we have zero.

'I have examined the bones under a microscope. One can

sometimes detect a gash caused by a knife. It's also sometimes possible to find a hairline fracture with no signs of healing. Other times, a breakage of the hyoid bone in the throat, which suggests strangulation. Here, we have none of these.

'What is extraordinary is how clean all these bones are. None of the torso, arms or upper leg bones is encased in muscle and ligament, putrefied or otherwise. There's no hair anywhere in the vicinity of the skull bones.

'What I can say is that this is, I believe, the skeleton of a young girl. I can't say, from the cranial or facial architecture, whether or not she was from Europe. But she's had no injury that I can see to her bones.

'This murderer, if there was one, knew what he or she was doing.'

'Just like a demonstrator in anatomy would know?' suggested Turnbull.

'Well, James, that's up your street not mine. Good luck.'

'Well, thank you, Professor. You and your team have done a great job as usual.'

'Thank you and so have the SOCO teams. It's now over to you to do your detective work. I'm due out for dinner.'

Turnbull and Jasper made their way to a pub in Adel where it was easy to park.

'What do you think?' asked Jasper.

'Well, I think it's her. Who else could it be? The absence of any signs of injury could mean she died naturally, but why would he bury her? He must have murdered her somehow, dissected the body and distributed the parts around the house, the garden, his office and his laboratory.'

'That would mean his wife must have known.'

'I agree,' said Turnbull. 'Of course, it's possible she killed her and he was her assistant, or they both did it together. But it's most likely him. He knows his way round bodies, she doesn't.'

'But where was it done?'

'We'll get Bill and his team to the house tomorrow. The chances are that he sawed her to bits somewhere in the house. He can't have cleaned every spot away. Bill will find it if there's any trace.'

'Could he have done it in his laboratory?'

'I suppose that's possible, but it's been used so much in the last six months that I doubt there'd be any trace of her left.'

'That's true,' said Jasper.

'Right,' said Turnbull. 'Let's get Bill on to it tomorrow.'

'It'll take his team days to report back.'

'So, let's meet up this evening at the usual pub. Ask the team along. They deserve it. Meanwhile, we've got to remember that the teeth are still missing.'

At 6:00 p.m. Turnbull and Jasper walked to the *Jacob's Well* pub in the centre of Bradford. They each got a pint and, within minutes, Roberts and Rowley arrived.

'Well done everyone,' said Turnbull. 'It's my shout, get whatever you want. There's a slate going. No talk about the current case in here. Remember, walls have ears.'

They got their drinks and settled around a corner table.

'Welcome back, Jane,' said Turnbull. Jane had been seconded to the Burglary Division for a few weeks while days were quiet. 'How did you get on with burglaries?'

'Nothing exciting,' said Jane. 'Burglaries of barns targeting farm equipment.'

'That reminds me of a case I was involved in when I was your age,' said Turnbull.

'Go on, sir, tell us. I love your stories.'

'Well, in the 1970s there was a spate of burglaries of mistals, that's the farm sheds where the cows were kept during the winter months. One mistal in particular seemed to be targeted. What was unusual was that an upturned bucket was found at the rear end of the same cow each time the mistal was broken into.

'After numerous break-ins we decided to install a burglar alarm in the mistal. At four o'clock in the morning, after the alarm had been installed, it went off. Another DC and I went post haste to the farm to check out the mistal.

'We entered the mistal and there again was the upturned bucket behind the same cow. The floor was covered with hay. We suspected our intruder was hiding in the hay so we each grabbed a pitchfork from the corner of the mistal and started prodding the hay with the two-pronged forks.

'After a few prods, a youth emerged from the hay with his hands up. He was covered from head to foot in straw and cow dung. *I give up*, he shouted. We arrested him for burglary with intent to commit an offence of sexual intercourse with a cow.

'*What's intercourse he asked?* Buggering a cow, I replied. *Didn't know it was illegal,* he said. Well, it's an offence under Section 69 of the Sexual Offences Act 2003 to have intercourse with a cow. We brought him to headquarters and interviewed him. *Daisy didn't mind,* he said. *I'm glad you caught me, my life's been a misery. I can't stop it.*

'I asked him why it was always the same cow. *That's the one I fancy,* he said. *I called her Daisy. You'll find I've got a record for burgling houses. The last time they sent me to borstal and they made me do PT in a field full of cows. You can imagine what effect that had on me. Getting a hard on when you're doing exercises.*

'I told him his secret was out and that we'd get him a duty solicitor. The solicitor arranged for a medical report from a psychiatrist at High Royds Hospital, then known locally as the Menston loony bin. He appeared at West Riding Quarter Sessions and his sentence was a probation order with a condition of treatment by the consultant at High Royds.'

'What was the treatment?' asked Jane.

'In those days, it was primitive. The psychiatrist put slides of cows on a screen and when he got a hard on, he gave him an electric shock.'

'God, did it work?'

'I don't know. Never heard of him after that.'

'Not surprised,' said Jane.

'Well,' said Turnbull. 'That's enough stories for today. Let's hope Bill Thornton has found something. Somehow, I doubt it.'

Chapter 14

The following day at five o'clock, Bill Thornton rang James Turnbull.

'We've examined every conceivable surface in that house; floors, flat surfaces, walls, skirting boards, dressing tables, et cetera. You name it, we've checked it and we've come up with absolutely nothing.'

'Nothing at all?'

'Zero. He can't have cut that body up in the house. Either that or he and his wife are the best cleaners I've ever come across in thirty years.'

'So, there's absolutely no way he dissected the body in the house?'

'No. I think it very unlikely. I think he must have done it out of hours in his laboratory at the University and there's no chance of finding anything there. That lab is used for dissection every day of the week and, at the end of each working day, it's thoroughly cleaned by professionals with chemicals. They have a special sluice to prevent body parts entering the normal sewerage system.'

'Have you any other ideas?'

'Not at the moment. See what Prof Talbot comes up with.'

'Okay, I'll give him a ring. Thanks Bill. Catch up with you later.'

'Good luck.'

* * *

Turnbull and Jasper went, by appointment, to see Professor Talbot in his laboratory at the University of Leeds.

'Prof, we've drawn a blank from forensics,' said Turnbull. 'Bill Thornton thinks the body was cut up somewhere other than the house. Jayasuriya's lab is the most likely place, but we've no chance of finding anything there. Of course, we have bones from the lab desk drawer et cetera, but that's all.'

'Well,' said Professor Talbot. 'I can tell you that the skeleton we have reconstructed exactly fits that of a teenage Sri Lankan girl and it fits the description of Fathima Mylvaganam. Who else could it be?'

'God only knows,' said Turnbull. 'We'll have to ask him. But if she was only murdered some months ago, how come there is no flesh attached to the bones?'

'Good question,' said Talbot. 'However, the flesh could more easily be disposed of, particularly by a demonstrator in anatomy. Flesh parts must be disposed of as a matter of routine in his lab.'

'That's true,' said Turnbull. 'Then our next task is to interview him. If you have any further thoughts, Prof, please get in touch.'

'I promise,' said Talbot. 'Find the teeth and we may get somewhere. If Doctor Jayasuriya comes up with any explanation, come back to me and I might be able to discredit it.'

'Will do. Many thanks.'

Turnbull and Jasper returned to their office.

Chapter 15

Turnbull and Jasper decided that now was the time to tackle Doctor Jayasuriya about the bones of the dead girl which were found in his house and at his laboratory. Also, about their discovery that he was her father. They arranged for him to attend Bradford police headquarters at noon the following day.

At precisely twelve noon, Doctor Jayasuriya arrived. He was accompanied by his solicitor, Richard Hodson. Once they were all seated in the interview room, where the tape recorder was turned on, those present identified themselves and James Turnbull addressed Doctor Jayasuriya.

'I am now going to interview you about Fathima Mylvaganam who is missing. You are not obliged to say anything when I question you. If, however, when questioned, it may harm your defence if you fail to mention any fact upon which you later rely on in Court.'

Richard Hodson interrupted. 'You should know, Mr Turnbull, that I have advised Dr Jayasuriya about adverse inference from silence and that I have advised my client not to answer any questions.'

'Thank you, Mr Hodson,' said Turnbull. 'You understand, Doctor Jayasuriya, that I am seeking to discover whether or not the offence of murder of Fathima Mylvaganam has been committed. By failing to assist me in answering questions about her disappearance, in any subsequent trial you may face, the Judge will direct the jury that such failure can harm any defence you may raise.'

'I understand that,' said Doctor Jayasuriya. 'All I will say is to repeat what I have said to you already and that is that, as far as I am concerned, she is still alive. She returned to Sri Lanka because her mother was taken ill.'

'How then do you explain the skeleton of a young girl, corresponding with Fathima's age, that's been recovered from your house, your garden, your laboratory and in places which indicate you intended to hide them?'

'I have no comment to make.'

'We have also discovered that you are Fathima's father. We have a copy of her birth certificate from Sri Lanka, which you are welcome to look at.'

Richard Hodson didn't look surprised at this revelation.

Jay examined the document and handed it back. 'I'm sorry I didn't mention this before, but my wife was present when you saw me and she doesn't know about it. But I can't see it makes any difference. She went home cos her mother was ill.'

'Doctor Jayasuriya, it makes a great deal of difference. Why did you seek her out and arrange for the agency to send her to you?'

'I wanted to see how she had grown up. When we wanted an au pair, it seemed the ideal opportunity to see her again. I've not seen her since birth. I wasn't intending to tell her or Tanoo that I was her father.'

'Why not? You'd arranged for her to come to the UK. Surely now was the time to tell her and Tanoo?'

'That wasn't my plan.'

'Are you sure you didn't tell her and she argued with you?'

'No, that's not what happened.'

'We have a witness who, one day in August, heard banging and shouting. What was that about?'

'I have no idea. I don't remember any such incident.'

'What obviously happened, we suggest, is that you murdered your daughter and then cut up her body and distributed it behind the garage, in plant pots in the house, in a holdall in the loft and at your workplace in your desk drawer.'

'No comment.'

'What possible reason can there be for dissecting a body in this way if it was not to hide the fact that you'd murdered her?'

'No comment.'

'Professor Talbot, the Forensic Pathologist, has reconstructed the skeleton. It corresponds exactly with what is known about her. However, you disposed of her teeth so that we could not identify her by reference to her dental records.'

'No comment.'

'You say she returned to Sri Lanka. Presumably she flew there.'

'No comment.'

'Yet extensive enquiries reveal that she never flew back to Sri Lanka.'

'No comment.'

'Did you ever see an airline ticket that she could've used to fly back?'

'No comment.'

'Had she any money to buy a ticket?'

'No comment.'

'We have recovered two hundred pounds in twenty pound notes from under her mattress. When you cleared up her possessions after murdering her, you failed to look under the mattress.'

'No comment.'

'There is no way that, if she left as you say, she would abandon her savings which she had secreted under her mattress.'

'No comment.'

'I assume you understand that legal advice to remain silent

cannot, by itself, prevent an adverse inference being drawn by a jury, otherwise the caution would be rendered wholly nugatory. The jury would not be concerned with the correctness of the advice, nor with whether it complies with the Law Society's guidelines. They would only be concerned about the reasonableness of your silence.'

'What does nugatory mean?'

'Meaningless, null and void.'

'I understand. I have no comment.'

'You are able to decide for yourself what you should do, despite whatever advice you have been given by Mr Hodson here.'

'I know that.'

'I have disclosed to you those facts upon which we rely and require an explanation from you.'

'I know that. However, I have decided to accept my solicitor's advice.'

'Very well, that concludes the interview. Thank you, Mr Hodson, for attending. If, in future, your client changes his mind and decides to give an explanation for the body parts we have found, please inform us and we will interview him again.'

They left the room and went their separate ways.

* * *

'Well, are you surprised at that turn of events?' Jasper asked Turnbull as they walked back to their office.

'Not really. If he came up with an explanation, he would know that we would have a good chance of discrediting it before trial. Whereas, as we are, we have little chance if the first time we hear of an explanation is at trial.'

'Yes, I understand that,' said Jasper. 'But surely he has to put in a defence statement?'

'That's true,' said Turnbull. 'But I expect it to say nothing save that the girl's alive. It's a funny one. Meanwhile, I'll submit the papers to the CPS to see whether or not they will recommend prosecution.'

Chapter 16

Myles Gibson, of the Crown Prosecution Service, received the papers sent by James Turnbull. He was the senior legal executive working for the CPS and had many years of experience. He found the case fascinating. He had dealt with many murders in his time with the CPS but none where the defence was that the victim was alive and well.

He was the preliminary sifting stage of the decision-making process. If he advised prosecution, it went up a level to the senior prosecutor in the CPS office in Leeds.

Myles knew that there existed a code which he must apply in determining whether proceedings for an offence could be justified, as recommended by James Turnbull. The code was on his wall in large print. He knew that every case had to be considered on its own merits: that a decision must be fair, independent and objective without regard for any personal views about ethnic or national origin: that his decision must not be taken as a result of pressure from the police: that the CPS must always act in the interests of justice – not solely for the purpose of obtaining a conviction. He knew it off by heart.

The code required that in the opinion of the CPS, the prospects of a successful prosecution were greater than those of failure, in other words that there is enough evidence to provide a realistic prospect of conviction. In Myles' opinion, the criteria were clearly established. There was a case of murder for Doctor Jayasuriya to answer.

He went upstairs to consult the senior CPS prosecutor. He knocked and was invited to enter his office. After pleasantries were exchanged, he explained the circumstances of the case to his boss.

The solicitor, Mr Ahmed, said: 'Well, I'm as satisfied as you are that there is a case to answer. However, Doctor Jayasuriya is a man of impeccable character. I think we should tread warily. Please arrange a consultation with Tom Beecroft QC and John Oldroyd. They work well for us as a team and this sounds just up their street. Keep the case under review in case our opinion changes.'

* * *

A week later, Myles Gibson went to Counsel's Chambers to see Beecroft and Oldroyd. He had sent the papers in advance to both Counsel and looked forward to the meeting. He had arranged for Turnbull and Jasper to meet him there.

They were ushered into Silks' (QC's) Conference Room, a huge high-ceilinged room with a large oblong conference table surrounded by a dozen or so chairs. Tea and biscuits were brought in and then Beecroft and Oldroyd entered.

Myles and the two police officers knew them well. They had last worked together on the *honour killing* case. Beecroft was a man is his fifties with quite long grey hair swept back from his face. He wore a bow tie. He had an air of authority and competence.

Oldroyd was in his late twenties and was wearing a black jacket and striped trousers. He had a reputation, as Beecroft's junior, for being very thorough.

'Good to see you all again,' said Beecroft. 'It doesn't seem long since the *honour killing*. How are things at the CPS Myles?'

'Cuts and more cuts. Fewer cases in which we instruct QCs for the prosecution in murder cases but this one's a bit odd and we thought we should instruct you both. Thank you for seeing us.'

'That's fine,' said Beecroft addressing Myles and the two police officers. 'It's not often I prosecute a murder case where the defence is that the alleged victim is still alive. It takes all sorts.'

'No, I agree,' said Turnbull. 'Never in my experience have I had such a case. He "no commented" in our interview with him so we don't know what his defence will be, if any.'

'I think there are three crucial factors in our favour,' said Beecroft. 'Firstly, the skeleton exactly matches the description of the missing girl. The absence of teeth shows something to hide.

'Secondly, there is no evidence that she flew back to Sri Lanka. Indeed, the contrary is the case. Her stepfather has had exhaustive enquiries made and there is no sign of her in Sri Lanka.

'And thirdly, the way the body was cut up and secreted in his garden, around the house and at his laboratory demonstrates a determination to hide her death. I can't for the life of me think what his defence is but I have no doubt that we should prosecute. We need statements from all the airlines which service Sri Lanka from the UK and European airports. I assume no shipping-line goes to Sri Lanka from British ports?'

'None that we could discover,' replied Turnbull.

'What concerns me more,' said Beecroft. 'Is whether we should prosecute his wife? You haven't interviewed her as yet.'

'No.'

'Well, the old rule that a wife cannot give evidence against her husband no longer applies. You may be able to nudge her in that direction. I doubt whether she'll say anything, but it's worth a try.'

'I'll see her tomorrow,' said Turnbull.

'The chances are that she will say nothing, just as her husband did,' said Beecroft. 'We could consider prosecuting her for murder or, alternatively, for obstructing the Coroner. Any disposition of a corpse with intent to obstruct or prevent a Coroner's inquest is a common law offence.

'But I wouldn't want to distract the jury from their main task of deciding whether murder is proved against her husband,' continued Beecroft. 'Unless she admits murder or concealment, my thoughts are not to prosecute her. Let Mr Oldroyd know how you get on interviewing her. If something significant happens, we'll meet again. Anything else?'

'No thanks, we'll keep you posted,' said Myles.

'I'll arrest Doctor Jayasuriya,' said Turnbull. 'Do we oppose bail?'

'Yes, I would. He's obviously a clever man and his roots here are tenuous,' replied Beecroft.

'I agree. Many thanks,' said Turnbull.

Turnbull, Jasper and Myles Gibson discussed the case further as they walked across Park Square.

'I'll set up the committal proceedings before the Magistrates. He is bound then to put in his defence statement and then we will know what his defence is,' said Myles.

'Hopefully, but don't bank on it,' said Turnbull as he and Jasper headed for their car and Myles to his office.

Chapter 17

The following morning, Turnbull and Jasper set off early for the Marriott Hotel on Hollins Hill, Baildon, to interview Mrs Jayasuriya. She was having breakfast with her husband and son, Venkat, when they arrived.

'I'm sorry to come so early,' said Turnbull. 'Venkat, can you leave us for a moment? Just go to reception and we'll come and get you when we've finished talking to your parents.

'We need to interview you, Mrs Jayasuriya, about the bones we found at your house. I suggest you have a different solicitor to your husband to advise you.

'So far as you are concerned, Doctor Jayasuriya, I arrest you for the murder of Fathima Mylvaganam. I understand from your interview that you have decided to say nothing so it's unnecessary to caution you again.

'If we wait in reception, could you be ready in half an hour? Doctor Jayasuriya, I suggest you bring a small suitcase with your night things and a change of clothes.'

The Jayasuriyas left the dining room and before returning to their room to pack, they went to reception to explain to Venkat what was happening and to make arrangements for him to be picked up by his aunt. Forty minutes later, the Jayasuriyas were transported to Bradford police headquarters.

Once they arrived there, and after a tearful goodbye to his wife, Doctor Jayasuriya was put in a cell. From there he was taken to Armley gaol where he would remain until his trial. His wife, Tanoo Jayasuriya, was taken to an interview room.

'We have a duty solicitor here today. It's a lady, Miss Patricia Lambert, are you happy if she advises you?' asked Turnbull.

'Yes,' she replied.

'In that case, I'll ask her to come to see you and we'll interview you in an hour or so, okay?'

'Yes, thank you.'

Chapter 18

'Now, Mrs Jayasuriya, I have turned on the tape recorder in order to record this interview. I am James Turnbull, Detective Chief Inspector, and with me is David Jasper, Detective Sergeant. With you is the duty solicitor, Miss Patricia Lambert, and you and she have been consulting for one hour before this interview began. Have you any questions so far?'

'No thank you.'

'At the beginning, I must caution you that you are not obliged to answer my questions but if you fail to mention, when questioned, something which you later rely on in Court, that may harm your defence.'

Miss Lambert interjected to say she had explained the caution to Mrs Jayasuriya and that she had also spoken, via telephone, to Richard Hodson who represented her husband.

'I don't know how you could think such horrible things,' said Mrs Jayasuriya. 'We loved Fathima. No one wanted to kill her. She was very happy here. She only left because her mother was ill.'

'How did she find out that her mother was ill?' asked Turnbull.

'I don't know. Maybe by telephone. Maybe she got a letter.'

'Did you see a letter?'

'No.'

When did she tell you that her mother was ill?'

'I can't remember.'

'She must have said how she'd heard.'

'I don't remember.'

'Had she even spoken before about her mother?'

'No, it came as a shock to her.'

'Did she go straight away?'

'Yes, she packed her things and left.'

'By taxi?'

'I don't know. We normally use Baildon Taxis. The number is on the board in the kitchen. I expect she used them.'

'Did she have a suitcase?'

'Yes and a haversack.'

'Had she any washing to collect?'

'I can't remember.'

'Did she say goodbye?'

'Yes, to me. Jay was at work.'

'So, she never said goodbye to Jay?'

'I don't think so.'

'You now know that he is Fathima's father?'

'Yes, he told me. It was a great shock.'

'Did she leave a note for her father?'

'I don't think so.'

'Well, if she had, surely he would have shown you it?'

'I expect so.'

'Do you know where she went when she left your house?'

'No.'

'To the bus station, the railway station, or Leeds Bradford Airport?'

'I don't know.'

'But she was a young teenager. Surely you were in *loco parentis* to her? That means in overall care of her wellbeing. Particularly as your husband is her father.'

'Well, she seemed determined to leave as soon as possible. She's a sensible girl. She'd flown here on her own. I was sure she could look after herself.'

'Did you hear her making any arrangements?'

'No.'

'What about money?'

'She said she had enough and that my husband had given her a hundred pounds, but I gave her fifty pounds.'

'You know, don't you, that we found two hundred pounds in twenty pound notes under her mattress? Also, she had two thousand pounds in a bank account at Barclays in Baildon and it's never been touched.'

'Yes, she must have left it there in a rush.'

'So that two hundred pounds wasn't your money?'

'No.'

'Who else could it belong to?'

'I don't know. We had visitors from Sri Lanka last year. It could be theirs.'

'Did they contact you to say they had lost it?'

'No.'

'Mrs Jayasuriya, we have reason to believe that Fathima was murdered and her body parts dissected and distributed around the house, the garden and your husband's place of work. What do you say about that?'

'I have nothing to say except that neither I nor Jay murdered her.'

'How do you explain body parts of a young woman being found in your house and garden?'

Miss Lambert intervened. 'You should know that I have advised Mrs Jayasuriya to follow her husband's example and answer no comment to all questions relating to this aspect of the case.'

'That's correct,' said Mrs Jayasuriya. 'I will do as my husband did and not answer any questions about your findings in the search.'

'Mrs Jayasuriya,' said Turnbull. 'You should know that if

you fail to answer my questions and subsequently give evidence in Court about the topic, your credibility may be damaged.'

'I understand that.'

'Also, that a solicitor's advice does not nullify the caution. It is up to you whether you answer the questions, not your solicitor; otherwise the caution would be meaningless.'

'I understand all that but my husband has made the decision. He's the head of our family and I will not answer any further questions on this topic.'

'Were you aware that your husband was putting bones in plant pots in your house?'

'No comment.'

'What possible reason could there be for putting bones there other than to hide them?'

'No comment.'

'Bones were found behind the garage. What do you know about them?'

'No comment.'

'And in a holdall in the loft?'

'No comment.'

'Surely you must have been aware that your husband was secreting the bones?'

'No comment.'

'Was there no unusual smell in the house?'

'No.'

'You do know the seriousness of your position?'

'Yes, of course I do, but Jay and I each have our own life to lead. I work and so does he. He is often at home on his own. I don't check on everything he does.'

'Were you not there when he was digging behind the garage?'

'I have no idea.'

'Well, Mrs Jayasuriya, thank you for coming in. Thank you, Miss Lambert. We will let you know whether any further action will be taken against Mrs Jayasuriya. Here's my card, Mrs Jayasuriya, you can contact me on this number day or night. It doesn't matter how trivial. Are you happy with that, Miss Lambert?'

'Yes.'

'Thank you,' said Mrs Jayasuriya. 'This is all so tragic.'

Turnbull announced that the interview was terminated and he switched off the tape recorder.

* * *

Turnbull and Jasper went back to their office.

'Dave, please send an email to Myles at the CPS. Tell him that nothing's been revealed in our interview with Mrs Jayasuriya and ask what his instructions are.'

'Okay, will do.'

'I find it hard to believe that she didn't know what was going on, but can we prove it? And, as Mr Beecroft said, will it detract from the main object of the trial, namely to nail her husband?''

'I agree,' said Jasper.

* * *

Later that day, after Oldroyd had replied by email, a decision was made not to prosecute Mrs Jayasuriya and her solicitor was informed of the decision in a letter from Myles Gibson of the CPS.

Chapter 19

The committal proceedings were held at Bradford Magistrates' Court one month later.

The CPS solicitor handed the statements and exhibits to the Court Clerk. Richard Hodson was asked by the Chairman of the Bench whether he or his client wished to say anything. Hodson replied not.

'Stand up, Doctor Jayasuriya. You are hereby committed to stand your trial for murder at Bradford Crown Court on the tenth of December. You will be remanded in custody.'

Richard Hodson stood and told the Bench he would be applying for bail to a Judge in chambers. But, in Turnbull's opinion, it would have little prospect of success. Bail is seldom granted in murder cases.

Jayasuriya was taken to the cells and thence to Armley gaol.

Turnbull spoke to Richard Hodson. 'Are you putting in a defence statement?'

'Yes, here it is,' he said as he handed it to Turnbull who read it out loud.

'Doctor Jayasuriya maintains no murder has been committed. His belief is that Fathima Mylvaganam is alive and well in Sri Lanka.

'Is that all?' asked Turnbull. 'What about an explanation for the bones?'

'Wait and see,' said Hodson with a smile.

Turnbull and Jasper returned to their office.

'The only thing we have learnt in these interviews, Dave, is that Fathima may have telephoned Baildon Taxis. Let's go and see them,' said Turnbull.

They went immediately to the office of Baildon Taxis located in the centre of the village.

'May we look at your records to see whether you sent a taxi to 22 Forest Hill, Baildon, between April and August of this year?'

'We should have that on the computer,' said the proprietor. 'Whose house is it?'

'Doctor Jayasuriya and his wife and child live there and they had an au pair called Fathima.'

'Oh yes, I know them. I'll put the address on the screen so we can look at it together.'

Up came the information.

'You can see for yourselves that the only taxi sent there was to go to the Alhambra in Bradford in June.'

'None to the airport, a railway station, or a bus station?' asked Turnbull.

'No. She may have gone with another firm, but I remember the girl. She used to use us from time to time to take her to a restaurant in Leeds. Her boyfriend would pay on arrival.'

'We'll require a statement from you at some point. We'll be in touch. Many thanks.'

'That's okay. Glad to help.'

* * *

'The mystery deepens. The bones must be hers. We have no trace whatsoever of her having left,' said Turnbull.

'I agree,' said Jasper.

'The failure to put in a meaningful defence statement will count against him at trial. If he comes up with an explanation, we may be chasing our tails trying to discredit it. I'll inform her stepfather of the trial date as he may want to come over.'

Chapter 20

The trial was set down at Bradford Crown Court before Mr Justice Griffiths. He came from London to try the case and would be staying at the Judges' lodgings on Stonegate Road in Leeds for the duration of the trial. There had been repeated controversy about the cost of maintenance of Judges' lodgings, but still they were used although allowed to fall into disrepair.

Court 6 at Bradford Crown Court was the largest courtroom in the building and was to be used in the event there was a large public interest in the case. The balcony would hold a hundred observers and in the well of the Court, there was enough room for about twenty journalists. The usual attendees were from the *Telegraph & Argus* and the *Yorkshire Post* but, in addition, there would probably be national and television interest.

The defence had instructed Mr Mountfield QC and Mr Blackstone. They were from Leeds Chambers and had been in the *honour killing* trial which had also been tried by Mr Justice Griffiths.

It's like a family reunion, thought Turnbull.

Thankfully, Fathima's stepfather had decided not to come over for the trial. He said he would find it too upsetting. He just wanted to be kept in touch and informed of events on a daily basis.

Chapter 21

The Court assembled ready for a 10:30 a.m. start. Waiting jurors stood at the back of the courtroom. From these men and women, twelve would be chosen to try Dr Jayasuriya.

Counsel entered Court, the Queen's Counsel (QCs) sat on the front row, Junior Counsel on the row behind and solicitors instructing Counsel on the row behind them. Thus, Myles Gibson sat behind Mr Oldroyd who sat behind Mr Beecroft QC and, for the defence, their solicitor, Richard Hodson, on the third row behind Junior Counsel for the defence, Mr Blackstone, who sat behind Mr Mountfield QC.

'All rise,' shouted the Court Usher. Everyone stood for the Judge, Mr Justice Griffiths, to enter. He bowed to the counsel's benches and sat down.

To Turnbull, who sat with Jasper on the row behind Myles Gibson, the Judge looked younger than he had done at the *honour killing* trial.

The remainder of the courtroom was packed. In the press box were reporters from the *Telegraph & Argus* and the *Yorkshire Post,* whom he recognised, as well as reporters from ITV's *Calendar*, BBC's *Look North* and those representing some of the national press.

In the public gallery, there were many Asian faces, *probably friends of Dr Jay's,* thought Turnbull. Mrs Jayasuriya was with them. As there was a possibility that she may be called as a witness, by the defence, the Court Usher asked her to kindly leave the courtroom. He explained that witnesses, who may give evidence themselves, are not permitted to sit in Court to listen to what is said before they give evidence. She appeared reluctant to leave, but did as she was asked.

Turnbull was surprised that Richard Hodson hadn't advised her of this beforehand, or maybe they had already decided not to call her as a witness for the defence, in which case she could have stayed in court.

Also in the public gallery was the usual band of regular viewers who came to Court week after week.

The Judge addressed Counsel, 'I assume we do not need an interpreter.'

'No, My Lord,' said Mr Mountfield.

'Will the defendant please stand,' said the Court Clerk. He was positioned at his desk, below the Judge, facing Counsel. He, like the Judge, and Counsel also wore a wig and gown. This was the tradition when the presiding Judge was a High Court Judge.

'Chaminda Jayasuriya, you are charged with murder and the particulars are that between the first of April 2008 and the first of August 2008, you murdered Fathima Mylvaganam. How do you plead, guilty or not guilty?' asked the Judge.

'Not guilty, My Lord,' said Dr Jayasuriya in a loud voice. He was smartly dressed in a grey suit with a white shirt and red tie. His hair was well-groomed in a close-cut style. He looked assured and calm as he sat with a prison officer on either side of him.

The Judge addressed the thirty or so jurors-in-waiting who were still standing patiently at the back of the courtroom.

'Ladies and gentlemen, twelve of you will try the defendant who is accused of murder.'

He then addressed Counsel, 'Will this case be finished within the two-week period which these jurors have agreed to sit?'

'Yes, My Lord,' replied Mountfield. 'My learned friend,

Mr Beecroft, and I have discussed this and we are confident the case will be finished within two weeks.'

'Very well,' said the Judge.

The Court Clerk then addressed the accused. 'Chaminda Jayasuriya, the names you will hear read out are those of the jurors who will try you. If you object to any one of them, your time to do so is before they come to the book to be sworn and before they are sworn, and your objection will be heard.'

Twelve men and women were then called one by one, by name, into the jury box. Each took the oath on the New Testament, saying, 'I swear by Almighty God that I will faithfully try the defendant and give a true verdict according to the evidence.'

Turnbull noted that there wasn't one Buddhist, Sikh or Jewish juror.

The jury were now formally in charge of the case and any verdict had to be theirs and theirs alone. Dr Jayasuriya's fate depended on them. If convicted of murder, there was only one possible sentence and that was life imprisonment. The minimum term he would serve would be a matter for the Judge.

The jury, surprisingly, comprised eight women and four men. Turnbull noticed that each juror had taken the oath with confidence, so he was satisfied that they could read and would listen carefully and return a well-considered verdict on the evidence presented before them by the prosecution and the defence.

The Court Clerk addressed the jury. 'Members of the jury, are you all sworn? Members of the jury, you have each taken an oath to try this defendant who is charged with murder. It is your task to say, having heard the evidence, whether he is guilty or not guilty.'

The Judge turned to the jury. 'It is now for leading Counsel for the prosecution to address you. May I, however, say this to you before he addresses you? This case may attract a lot of publicity. Please, during the trial, do not read any newspaper articles about it nor listen to or watch recordings on the radio or television about it. The reason is that you decide this case on the evidence you hear in court and on no other basis. It follows that you must not make any enquiries on the internet.

'Now you will listen to Mr Beecroft who will outline the prosecution case.'

Mr Beecroft stood, bowed to the Judge and then faced the jury.

'May it please your Lordship, members of the jury, as you have heard, Chaminda Jayasuriya is charged with the murder of Fathima Mylvaganam, a seventeen-year-old Sri Lankan girl who was employed by the Jayasuriyas as an au pair for their son.

'The Crown alleges that she was murdered by the defendant, Chaminda Jayasuriya. How she was murdered is not known, but murdered she was. After she was murdered, her body parts were secreted by Dr Jayasuriya in his house, his garden and in his laboratory at his place of work.

'Dr Jayasuriya is a qualified doctor, a man of hitherto unblemished character and a lecturer in medicine at Leeds University. That job involves his also being a demonstrator in human anatomy. The Crown's case is that this expertise enabled him to dispose of the body of Fathima Mylvaganam whom he had murdered.

'It is my task, together with my learned friend Mr Oldroyd, to present the prosecution case to you. You decide the case on the evidence, not on what I say. My sole purpose, at this stage, is to set out a framework of the case into which you can fit the evidence when it is called.

'The defendant is represented by my learned friends, Mr Mountfield QC, and Mr Blackstone who sit here beside and behind me.

'The story begins, so far as the Crown is concerned, in March 2008 when Dr Jayasuriya was living with his wife, Tanoo, and their ten-year-old son, Venkat, in a detached bungalow in the village of Baildon just outside Shipley. Their next-door neighbours were John and Liz Campbell whose house was also a bungalow.

'From time-to-time, as neighbours do, John and Jay, which was the name Dr Jayasuriya often went by, would chat over the hedge that separated their gardens. Their relationship could be described as a typically neighbourly one.

'In March 2008, Fathima Mylvaganam came to stay with the Jayasuriya family as their au pair. She was employed to look after their ten-year-old son, Venkat. Tanoo Jayasuriya worked at a garden centre near Otley and so needed help looking after Venkat, particularly in the school holidays.

'We also now know that the defendant, Doctor Chaminda Jayasuriya, was Fathima's father from a relationship before he married nearly fifteen years ago. It was he who, through an agency, found Fathima and made arrangements for her to come to the UK as their au pair. Fathima, it appears, did not know Doctor Jayasuriya was her father, nor did his wife.

'Fathima seemed to enjoy her job and frequently, during school holidays, went with Venkat to the Campbell's house so that Venkat could play cricket with Henry, the Campbell's nine-year-old son. She would chat to Liz whilst the boys played and sometimes she would help Liz with the housework.

'Then, in April, or thereabouts, she was not to be seen. The Campbells, not wishing to pry, let weeks pass whilst feeling that her disappearance was very odd. John Campbell also saw less of Dr Jayasuriya as he appeared to have stopped gardening.

'However, one day, John saw Dr Jayasuriya in the driveway and he asked him where he'd been and what had happened to Fathima. Dr Jay said he had been busy at work and that Fathima had returned to Sri Lanka because her mother was ill.

'That evening, John and Liz discussed this explanation and, not being satisfied, asked locals what they knew. Fathima's boyfriend, Phillip Green, said she had just stood him up without explanation. Her English teacher said she had just stopped attending classes. She had seemingly not told anyone she was leaving, nor that her mother was ill.

'So, the Campbells decided to report her disappearance to the police. Police enquiries made to all the airlines showed no sign of Fathima being on any flight from the UK to Sri Lanka.

'After further negative results from even more enquiries, her disappearance was reported by Missing Persons to the Murder Squad in the person of Detective Chief Inspector Turnbull.

'His team found no trace of any of her belongings in the Jayasuriya's house, except for one thing. Two hundred pounds in twenty pound notes was recovered from under her mattress. They thought that the chances of her forgetting to take her savings with her, when leaving, were remote. Whoever had removed her possessions had not checked under the mattress. Also, she had two thousand pounds in a bank account with Barclays in Baildon and that remained untouched.

'This led to the police deciding, as a first step, to apply for a search warrant. This they obtained and a systematic search began of the Jayasuriya house, garden and Dr Jayasuriya's workplace.

'Behind the garage, buried in rough ground, they found bones. A forensic pathologist was called to the scene and he confirmed that the bones were from a human being. The search of the rest of the garden revealed nothing.

'However, inside the house, they found bones in three plant pots in the hall and in a holdall in the loft. All were confirmed to be human bones.

'In Dr Jay's desk in his laboratory at Leeds University, more bones were found in formalin. When asked for an explanation, Dr Jay said: *no comment.*

'Even to this day, Dr Jay has offered no explanation. In his defence statement put in before the trial, all he has said is that Fathima is still alive.

'I'm afraid, ladies and gentlemen, that is a lie and he knows it. Fathima's bones were hidden in his house, the garden and at his place of work after he had murdered her. The eminent pathologist, Professor John Talbot, and his team have reconstructed a skeleton from the bones recovered and it is that of a teenage girl.

'The Crown submits they are the bones of Fathima Mylvaganam and that she was murdered by Dr Chaminda Jayasuriya, her employer.

'We will now call the evidence to prove it. I call John Campbell.'

There was a hubbub in Court whilst everyone settled down to listen to the evidence. John Campbell walked into Court and into the witness box. He took the bible in his right hand and repeated the oath after the Court Usher's prompting.

'I swear by Almighty God that the evidence I shall give will be the truth, the whole truth and nothing but the truth.'

'Please state your full name,' ordered Mr Beecroft.

'John Edward Campbell.'

'And your occupation?'

'I am a contract gardener.'

'And where do you live?'

'Twenty-two Forest Hill, Baildon.'

'And is your next door neighbour the defendant, Chaminda Jayasuriya?'

'Yes, he is, together with his wife and their son, Venkat.'

'Do you remember Fathima Mylvaganam arriving as their au pair?'

'Yes, I do, in March this year.'

'Did you meet her?'

'Yes. Tanoo, Dr Jayasuriya's wife, brought her round, with Venkat. She wanted to introduce Fathima to my wife, Liz, and our son, Henry, who is nine years old.'

'Will you describe your impression of Fathima.'

'Yes, she was in her teens, slightly plump. She was shy at first but she soon became relaxed. She spoke good English for a girl of that age. She appeared to be happy in her environment and seemed to get on with Venkat, her charge, who of course knew our son, Henry.'

'How often did you see her?'

'She came round at least twice a week over the following eight or so weeks so that Venkat could play cricket with Henry. I was at work most of the early weeks, but I sometimes saw her when I got home.'

'And how was she?'

'Very happy. Always smiling and laughing. She was a very nice, bright young girl. One afternoon, I heard shouting from next door, but I don't know who it was.'

'And then?'

'Well, she just stopped coming. We all missed her, but presumed there would be a good reason for it.'

'Did you ask your neighbour about her?'

'Yes, I saw Jay one day and asked him if Fathima was alright as we hadn't seen her. I also asked him where he had been as we hadn't seen him around for quite a while either.'

'What did he say?'

'He said Fathima had gone back to Sri Lanka because her mother was ill.'

'Did he say why he hadn't been around?'

'Yes, he said he had been very busy at the University. He was doing more demonstrating in anatomy. Someone in the department was ill and he was taking on a greater workload.'

'Did he ever tell you that he was the girl's father?'

'No, never.'

'What happened next?'

'Well, I discussed what he had said with my wife, Liz. We didn't want to seem like interfering neighbours but we were concerned for her wellbeing. You see, she told Liz that her parents were separated or divorced and that she was very close to her stepfather but didn't see her mother. So it struck us as very odd that she would be rushing back to Sri Lanka to take care of her mother. Anyway, we decided to ask around as to what impression others had got.'

'Do you play cricket for Baildon?'

'Yes, I do. I am the eldest in the team. We have mostly younger players.'

'And is one of the younger players Phillip Green?'

'Yes.'

'Did you speak to him?'

'Yes.'

The Judge intervened. 'Mr Mountfield, what Phillip Green said is necessarily hearsay evidence. However, I understand we are to hear from Mr Green. Have you any objection to this evidence?'

'No, My Lord,' replied Mountfield.

'Very well, continue Mr Beecroft,' said the Judge.

'Mr Campbell,' said Mr Beecroft. 'What did Phillip Green say to you?'

'He asked me whether I knew what had happened to Fathima as he knew that I lived next door to the Jayasuriyas. I told him she had gone back to Sri Lanka because her mother was ill. He couldn't understand why she hadn't been in touch with him. She'd just stood him up and disappeared.'

'I decided, after speaking to Phillip Green and after my wife told me what her enquiries had revealed, to report Fathima as a missing person.'

'And then?'

'The following Monday morning, Liz and I went to Shipley Police Station and reported it.'

'After that, were you visited by a uniformed police constable?'

'Yes, we were.'

'I have no more questions,' said Beecroft.

'Have you any cross-examination, Mr Mountfield?' asked the Judge.

'Yes, My Lord,' replied Mr Mountfield. 'Your relationship with Dr Jayasuriya was purely a neighbourly one?'

'Yes.'

'You were never friends?'

'No.'

'You didn't confide in him, nor did he confide in you?'

'No.'

'And the same applies to Fathima. She was a teenager who happened to live next door?'

'Yes.'

'You, indeed, seldom spoke to her?'

'That's correct.'

'But when you saw her, she seemed happy and contented?'

'Yes, I would say so.'

'No more questions, My Lord.'

John Campbell left Court. There was an air of anticipation as to who would be called next.

* * *

'The Crown call Elizabeth Campbell,' said Mr Oldroyd, Junior Counsel for the Crown.

A smart, confident lady walked into the Court and took the oath.

'Are you Elizabeth Campbell?' asked Mr Oldroyd.

'Yes, I am.'

'The wife of the last witness, John Campbell?'

'Yes.'

'You remember Fathima?'

'Yes, very well.'

'What was your first impression?'

'She was a kind, bubbly girl who seemed to settle in very well next door. She used to come round to our house with Venkat who liked to play cricket with Henry, when it was light enough, or they'd play inside. Venkat was teaching Henry to play Cluedo. Whilst the boys were playing, Fathima and I would have a cup of tea or coffee and have a chat. Occasionally she would help me with some of the housework.'

'When you were having these chats, did she ever speak of her parents?'

'Yes, she lived with her stepfather who had given his blessing for Fathima to come here. Even though she was only a teenager, he was happy for her to be living with a reputable Sri Lankan family so that she could improve her English and also learn to be independent. Her mother and stepfather were no longer together and she didn't see her mother.'

'And how often did she visit you?'

'At least twice a week, but then she just stopped coming for no apparent reason.'

'Did you speak to the defendant about that?'

'No, but my husband did.'

'In time, did you and your husband go to the Shipley Police Station to report that she was missing?'

'Yes, we did. We weren't sure about what to do. This seemed to be the best course of action.'

'Thank you, Mrs Campbell, I have no more questions.'

'Any cross-examination, Mr Mountfield?' asked the Judge.

'Yes, My Lord, if I may. How many times in all did Fathima visit your house?'

'It's difficult to be exact, one to two dozen times.'

'For how long each time?'

'About two hours at the most.'

'Did you see her in the company of Dr Jayasuriya?'

'Yes, I did, several times.'

'Did there seem to be any friction between them?'

'No, on the contrary, she seemed very relaxed in his company.'

'Thank you, My Lord, no more questions.'

Mr Beecroft stood. 'Next, My Lord, Mr Oldroyd will call a number of witnesses whose paths crossed with Fathima,' he said.

Oldroyd stood from the row behind Beecroft.

'My Lord, I call Fiona Wilson.'

The witness came into Court, avoiding looking at the dock. She took the oath.

'What is your full name?'

'Fiona Wilson.'

'And your occupation?'

'School teacher.'

'What is your subject?'

'English language and English literature.'

'And do you hold classes at the Ian Clough Hall, Baildon, for foreign students wanting to learn English?'

'I do.'

'And was Fathima Mylvaganam one such student?'

'Yes, sir, she was.'

'What was your impression of her?'

'Bright, anxious to learn.'

'Did she seem worried at all?'

'On the contrary, she seemed very happy.'

'Did you speak to her outside class?'

'Yes, several times.'

'To what effect.'

'She said she was anxious to improve her English. She wanted to stay in Baildon.'

'Did she speak of her parents?'

'Yes, she spoke affectionately about her stepfather but never spoke of her mother except to say that her parents were divorced, which I understand is quite unusual in Sri Lanka.'

'Did she ever say her mother was ill?'

'No, she just never mentioned her mother at all. When she was in Sri Lanka, she lived with her stepfather.'

'Did she pay for her English classes?'

'Yes, she paid cash in advance.'

'Then she stopped attending?'

'Yes, without any notice. She had paid for twelve classes, but only attended four.'

'Could she have had a refund if she had approached you and told you she didn't want to continue with the classes?'

'Well, not formally. But if she had said her mother was ill and she had to return to Sri Lanka, I would have made an exception and repaid her two-thirds of the fee.'

'I have no more questions,' said Mr Oldroyd.

'I think we will have a comfort break for fifteen minutes,' said the Judge.

The Judge and jury retired. Turnbull and Jasper retired to the Police Room.

'What do you think?' asked Jasper.

'Well, the defence is painting the picture of a happy girl who had a good relationship with her employer, Dr Jayasuriya, thereby setting their platform that he had no reason to murder her.'

'I see that, but wait for the airline evidence. I think that's crucial,' said Jasper.

* * *

Court reassembled after the break. Mr Mountfield stood to cross-examine.

'Did you ever tell her that if she failed to attend, she could get a rebate?'

'No, I didn't.'

'Have you ever before given a rebate?'

'No.'

'How many students were in her class?'

'Twelve.'

'Were you, in any way, close to any of your students?'

'No, that was not the nature of our relationship.'

'If your mother was ill, would you mention that to any of your students?'

'No. Unless I had to cancel a class for that reason, then I may.'

'I have no more questions.'

'Next, My Lord,' said Oldroyd, 'I call Malcolm Slingsby.'

Mr Slingsby entered the witness box wearing the uniform of Emirates Airlines.

'Your name please?'

'Malcolm Slingsby.'

'Your occupation?

'I work for Emirates Airlines in the ticket department. I am also air co-ordinator for airlines to and from Sri Lanka.'

'What does that job entail?'

'I have access to all the computer records of all the airlines flying to and from Sri Lanka to the UK.'

'Which airlines does that cover?'

'That covers Emirates, Oman Air, British Airways, Etihad, Qatar Airways and KLM.'

'Did you access your computer records for a passenger called Fathima Mylvaganam?'

'Yes, I did.'

'With what result?'

'She flew into Heathrow from Colombo on the second of March 2008 with Emirates.'

'Can you say whether or not she had a return ticket?'

'Yes, she did. She had an open return ticket.'

'So, her return fare was paid for?'

'Yes, it was.'

'Was it ever used?'

'Not according to our records.'

'With such a ticket, what does a passenger do?'

'If the passenger wishes to use the return portion of the ticket, he or she must book a flight. When that's done, the passenger attends for the flight check-in in the usual way. They are then given a boarding pass, which is checked at the gate, and the passenger boards the plane.'

'Is it possible that the passenger used her ticket without the airline having a record of her doing so?'

'No.'

'I have no further questions.'

Mr Mountfield stood for cross-examination.

'So this passenger had a valid ticket?'

'Yes.'

'Which had been paid for?'

'Yes.'

'Are mistakes never made at your company?'

'Of course there are, but for her to board the plane without any record of it would involve numerous mistakes. A mistake at the booking office, a mistake at the check-in, a mistake at the gate and a mistake on boarding. I consider that impossible.'

'I have no more questions,' said Mr Mountfield.

'Any re-examination, Mr Beecroft?' asked the Judge.

'No, My Lord.'

'I consider that to be an appropriate moment to adjourn until tomorrow. Remember my warning, members of the jury. Please be back to commence at 10:30 tomorrow morning. You may now go,' said the Judge.

The jury retired.

'All rise,' said the Court Clerk. Everyone rose to their feet, Counsel bowed and the Judge withdrew.

'Let's get out,' said Turnbull. 'That was good. We need to celebrate.'

He and Jasper went to the Jacob's Well. Jasper got the drinks and they made their way to the quietest corner of the pub.

'Let's think this through,' said Jasper. 'That evidence confounds the defence that she flew home because her mother was ill. She didn't get a taxi from Baildon Taxis. She could have got on the train to London. She had an open return ticket and never used it. If she was going home, she would have used her ticket. Game over.'

'Let's hope so,' said Turnbull.

* * *

The following morning, the Court reassembled. The jury came in and sat patiently.

'All rise,' said the Clerk.

The Judge came in and bowed to Counsel who bowed back.

'My Lord,' we now call Phillip Green,' said Mr Oldroyd.

A smart young man, wearing a blazer and tie, walked swiftly into Court. He was about six feet two inches tall and had long curly hair. Turnbull thought he had the build of a fast bowler, rather like Sidebottom, the Yorkshire and England bowler. He took the oath.

'What is your full name?' asked Oldroyd.

'Phillip Allan Green, sir,' he replied respectfully.

'How old are you?'

'Nineteen, sir.'

'And your occupation?'

'I'm a student.'

'Where at?'

'Sheffield University, reading geography.'

'Did you know Fathima Mylvaganam?'

'Yes, for a few weeks.'

'Where did you meet her?'

'In a pub in Baildon. She was drinking with some Sri Lankan friends and we got chatting.'

'How was she?'

'Well, bubbly, enjoying herself.'

'And did you ask her out?'

'Yes, for the following Saturday. That was her day off.'

'And what did you do?'

'I collected her from Forest Hill and we went to a Sri Lankan restaurant in Leeds, which she seemed to frequent regularly. It's a Sri Lankan students' haunt.'

'What happened thereafter?'

'Well, we went out a few times. Once I went with her to a Sri Lankan Society meeting at the Polish Club in Bradford. I considered her to be my girlfriend. I really liked her and enjoyed her company.'

'How did all this end?'

'She just stood me up. I went to collect her one Saturday, as arranged, and I was told she had gone. Her employer said she had gone back to Sri Lanka because her mother was ill.'

'Had she ever talked to you about her mother?'

'No, never. I thought it was very strange.'

'Thank you, no more questions.'

'Any questions, Mr Mountfield?' asked the Judge.

'Yes, My Lord. Mr Green, isn't describing Fathima as your girlfriend something of an exaggeration?'

'I suppose so.'

'I mean, did you ever kiss her?'

'No, we hadn't got that far.'

'And you went out together for what, six times in all?'

'About that.'

'No more questions.'

The Crown then called evidence of the search and the finding of bones. The defence had no questions.

'I call Professor Talbot,' said Mr Beecroft.

Professor Talbot took the oath with the customary

confidence of an expert witness.

'My name is John Talbot. I am the Professor in Forensic Pathology at the University of Leeds.'

'Professor, were you called to the scene of a suspicious death at number 22 Forest Hill, Baildon, on the fourth of August 2008?'

'I was.'

'And did you meet there Detective Chief Inspector James Turnbull and the Scenes of Crime Officer Bill Thornton?'

'I did.'

'Did they show you a hole dug in the garden behind the garage?'

'They did and I saw human bones there. On first impression, they appeared to be bones from the hands, feet and neck of a human being.'

'Was any flesh or other human matter attached to the bones?'

'No, they were completely clean.'

'Did you attend for a second time the following day?'

'Yes, I did.'

'And were you shown a holdall, a food container and three plant pots?'

'I was. In the holdall, which I understand was recovered from the loft, I saw bones from two femurs, tibias and fibulas, in other words the leg bones. Also, the left and right humerus, the arm bones.'

'What did you find in the plant pots?'

'Bones from the spine.'

'Were you shown a kitchen container?'

'Yes, I was. In the container were bones from the hands.'

'Later that day, did you attend Dr Jayasuriya's laboratory and office at the university?'

'Yes, I did. In a large coffee jar in the biology laboratory I saw bone from the skull and cheek kept in formalin.'

'And in a steel tray, also in the lab?'

'I saw two radius and ulna bones which are the arm bones, as well as jaw and skull bones.'

'And in the green beaker?'

'A sacroiliac joint, that's a hip bone.'

'And in a desk drawer?'

'Some bones from the skull.'

'Were these all recovered by your laboratory team?'

'They were and they reconstructed the bones to form the human skeleton.'

'Were any bones missing?'

'Yes, some ribs, one femur and some small bones from the ankles and feet.'

'When all these bones were put together, as it were, did they all appear to come from the same skeleton?'

'Yes, they did. I didn't see anything to indicate that they were from more than one person.'

'And was that person male or female?'

'Female and I would estimate from a young woman who had just ceased growing.'

'How tall was she?'

'About five feet six inches tall.'

'Could you judge anything else about her?'

'No, except that there were no signs of any of the bones being injured, for example there were no signs of knife damage. However, the absence of the ribs meant that she could, for example, have been stabbed in the chest and the rib bones damaged. One often sees a nick in the bone if that has happened.'

'Were you able to tell how long the bones had been in situ?'

'Judging by their cleanliness, not for more than a few months but it's impossible to be more specific.'

'Thank you, Professor, I have no more questions.' Mr Beecroft sat down.

Mr Mountfield stood to cross-examine.

'Am I correct in understanding that there was no way of identifying whose skeleton this was?'

'Correct, it was the skeleton of any girl of that age.'

'Nor could you determine, from what you saw, the ethnic origin of the girl?'

'Correct, she could have been white, black, Asian or a mixed race.'

'What else was missing?'

'Her teeth had all been extracted. Certainly, no teeth were found.'

'If they had been found, would identification of the body have been easier?'

'Yes, if the skeleton is said to belong to a particular person, as I understand to be the case, then if her dental records had been recovered, it may have been possible to identify her from those.'

'And no human tissue of any kind was attached to the bones?'

'That's correct.'

'Professor, how do you know it wasn't a man?'

'Even I can tell a man from a woman.' There was laughter in Court.

'I'm sure you can, but does the skeleton of a woman differ from that of a man?'

'Yes, the pelvis is a different shape.'

'And how do you know she was post pubertal?'

'By her pelvic notch. I can see from that that she had begun menstruating.'

'So, this could be the skeleton of a girl of between thirteen and twenty years of age?'

'That's correct. It's not possible to be more exact.'

'Now, is it possible to date the death?'

'No, I can't say save that the appearance of the bones suggested a recent death.'

'But it could be that the bones were kept clean for years, couldn't they?'

'Yes, that's true.'

'Can we just establish what you didn't find? There was an absence of dental history of Fathima Mylvaganam?'

'Yes.'

'So there were no teeth to check against her dental records?'

'Correct.'

'And you examined all the bones under a microscope?'

'Yes.'

'If there had been a gash caused by a knife, you would have detected it?'

'Yes.'

'But there was none?'

'Correct.'

'And if the hyoid bone had been broken, that would have suggested strangulation?'

'Yes.'

'But there was no such fracture?'

'No.'

'Nor was there any hair recovered?'

'No.'

'Nor clothing?'

'None.'

'What was unusual is that these bones were totally clean,

is that so?'

'Yes.'

'There was no muscle, no ligament anywhere?'

'Correct.'

'So, there is nothing on the skeleton which raises suspicions that this death was as a result of murder?'

'Correct.'

'She wasn't strangled, she wasn't stabbed and she wasn't bashed on the head?'

'Correct.'

'And those are the most common ways in which a murder is committed?'

'Correct.'

'May I, Professor, now ask you some general questions about the human skeleton? I suggest it's not always easy to tell the sex of skeletal remains?'

'I agree.'

'I suggest that recognizable sex differences do not appear until after puberty?'

'I agree.'

'That's the interval between fifteen and twenty years, is it not?'

'Yes, that's right.'

'Up to that time, am I right that the skeleton of the two sexes differs only in size?'

'Correct.'

'Also, the size differences due to sex are easily confused with those due to race and nutrition?'

'Correct.'

'So, it's not often obvious that the skeleton under examination is post-adolescent in size? Thus, there is a wide variation in the normal?'

'I agree.'

'And the retardation of growth can create a confusing picture?'

'Yes.'

'This can be caused by a variety of factors including race, fresh air, ultra-violet light and exercise. So, sexing a skeleton can be extremely difficult for all these reasons?'

'Yes.'

'And, judging the age, is even more difficult?'

'Yes.'

'In this instant, you had only the skeleton to examine?'

'Yes.'

'All the organs and soft tissue were absent?'

'Yes.'

'So, it was impossible to determine with any exactitude the age of this skeleton?'

'I would say it was between fifteen and twenty years of age at death.'

'Can you be sure that this was the skeleton of a girl?'

'My examination of the pelvis, the sternum, the skull and the long bones suggested that this was the skeleton of a girl.'

'How often, in your career, have you had to sex and age skeletal remains?'

'Many times.'

'Would you agree that it is only after the age of seventeen years that male characteristics begin to develop?'

'Yes.'

'So, up to that age, it is often extremely difficult, if not impossible, to sex a skeleton?'

'I agree.'

'As to age, external inspection of the dead permits only an approximate estimate of age?'

'Yes.'

'And it is liable to error by up to ten years when the subject is an adult?'

'Yes.'

'You have given an estimate of the height of this skeleton. At best, however, your estimate can be no more than an approximation?'

'I agree.'

'How many skeletons of Sri Lankans have you examined?'

'Before this, none.'

'Thank you, Professor, I have no more questions,' said Mr Mountfield who then sat down.

Mr Beecroft indicated that he had no re-examination.

'We'll adjourn now until tomorrow,' said the Judge. 'Members of the jury, no talking please to anyone outside your own number and if you do talk between yourselves, please do so in the privacy of your jury room.'

'All stand,' said the Court Clerk. Everyone stood and Counsel bowed to the Judge who withdrew, as did the jury.

Turnbull turned to Jasper. 'Let's get out before the rush.'

On the walk back to headquarters, Turnbull and Jasper discussed the day's events. 'Let's go to Jacob's Well for a pint,' said Turnbull.

'Good idea,' replied Jasper.

Turnbull bought two pints of Tetley's bitter and some pork scratchings. They sat at a wooden table in the corner of the pub.

'What do you think?' asked Turnbull.

'Well, it seems as though the issue is going to be the identification of the body.'

'I agree,' said Turnbull. 'But what is it doing hidden and if it isn't Fathima's, how come there's no trace of her flying back to Sri Lanka, or anywhere else for that matter?'

'I agree, it must be her.'

'Let's hope the jury come to that conclusion, but you never know. There are ways of getting out of the country without anyone knowing.'

'Yes, but that would apply to people who are criminals or illegals, surely not to a teenage au pair girl,' said Jasper.

'I think Jayasuriya's going to come up with some fanciful explanation for the skeleton,' said Turnbull. 'The Judge can direct the jury 'til the cows come home on how doing that can harm his defence, but whether they will take it on board is anyone's guess.'

'Let's go home. I'll see you tomorrow for another day of excitement in Court,' said Jasper.

'I agree, Dave,' said Turnbull. 'My wife has promised me fresh plaice tonight. It's our anniversary.'

'Oh, that's nice. Happy anniversary. Have a lovely evening,' said Jasper as they left the pub and walked across to headquarters in the rain.

Chapter 22

The Court reassembled at 10:30 a.m. The jury entered and sat patiently.

'All rise,' called the Court Clerk. Everyone rose to their feet and the Judge entered the courtroom. Counsel bowed to the Judge.

'My Lord, next we call SOCO Bill Thornton.'

Officer Thornton made his way to the witness box with his file tucked under his arm. He took the oath and faced Mr Beecroft.

'Please state your full name and occupation.'

'I am William Thornton, a senior Scenes of Crime Officer.'

'How many years of experience do you have?'

'Twenty years.'

'And were you the Scenes of Crime Officer in charge during the search of Doctor Jayasuriya's house and grounds and at his place of work?'

'Yes, I was.'

'Please describe what you found in the house and garden.'

'We found human bones buried behind the garage.'

'Did you find any bones elsewhere in the grounds of the house?'

'No. Nothing else was found during a dig of the whole garden by a team of thirty men.'

'On the following day, did your team conduct a search and examination of the house?'

'Yes, as shown in the exhibit, we found bones in three plant pots in the hall; a container in the kitchen and a holdall in the loft.'

'And all these were labelled and sent on to Professor Talbot?'

'Yes.'

'Did you search for blood stains in the house?'

'Yes, we examined every conceivable surface with no positive result.'

'Did you conclude that it was unlikely the body was cut up in the house?'

'Yes.'

'Thank you, no more questions.'

The Judge addressed Mr Mountfield. 'Any questions, Mr Mountfield?'

'Yes, one, if I may,' said Mountfield. 'If there had been the alleged victim's blood in the house, you would have found it?'

'I think there's a ninety-nine percent chance we would've done.'

'Thank you.'

Officer Thornton withdrew.

'My Lord,' said Mr Beecroft. 'Next, we call the officer in overall charge of the case, Detective Chief Inspector James Turnbull.'

James entered the witness box and took the oath on the New Testament.

'Your full name and rank please.'

'James Turnbull, Detective Chief Inspector, Bradford Homicide Squad.'

'How did you first become involved with this case?'

'I received a report from Missing Persons that a young Sri Lankan girl, Fathima Mylvaganam, had gone missing. She had supposedly gone back to Sri Lanka because her mother was ill but checks with all the airlines which serve Sri Lanka, could find no trace of her returning.'

'So, what did you do?'

'Well, we questioned known associates of Fathima's and received no positive feedback, so we went to question the accused and his wife.'

'What did they say?'

'That she had returned to Sri Lanka because her mother was ill.'

'Did you ask to look at her bedroom?'

'Yes, we conducted a thorough search. There was no trace of any personal belongings, except for a toothbrush. But, under the mattress, we recovered two hundred pounds in twenty pound notes.'

'Did you ask the accused about the money?'

'Yes, he said the money could have been Fathima's or that of a Sri Lankan friend of theirs who visited before Fathima went to live with them. But, after questioning, he said the visitor had never telephoned to say he had left any money behind. We assumed, therefore, that it was Fathima's money.'

'What next?'

'Well, we followed up on previous enquiries and spoke to Fiona, Fathima's English teacher; her male friend, Phillip Green; and the zebra crossing lady. Then we decided to apply for a search warrant of Doctor Jayasuriya's house.'

'And then?'

'I got a team together of thirty searchers. On day one, we dug the garden and behind the garage we found the bones which Professor Talbot subsequently identified as being bones from hands, feet and neck.

'On day two, we thoroughly searched the house. We found bones buried in three plant pots in the hallway; in a container in the kitchen and in a holdall in the loft. All these bones were identified by Professor Talbot as being human bones.'

'What next?'

'On day three, we made a thorough search of Doctor Jayasuriya's work place at Leeds University. In the biology laboratory we found bones in a coffee jar, a steel tray and in a beaker. We also found bones in his desk drawer.'

'Did you arrange an interview with Doctor Jayasuriya, with his solicitor present?'

'Yes.'

'Did you caution him to say that if he failed to mention something he later relied on in Court, it could harm his defence?'

'Yes and his solicitor said he had advised him to *no comment.*'

'And did he do so?'

'Yes, with the odd exception.'

'And do you produce a transcript of all questions and answers?'

'Yes.'

Copies of the questions and answers were then distributed to the jury.

'My Lord, do you wish me to take the witness through the interview?'

'No, but I think we should allow the jury a few minutes to read the transcript.'

'If your Lordship pleases.'

The jury then read the transcript, after which Mr Beecroft continued.

'Did you put to him that he was the girl's father?'

'Yes, he admitted such. He said that neither his wife nor Fathima knew.'

'Subsequently, did you charge Doctor Jayasuriya with murder and did he make no reply?'

'Yes.'

'Thank you,' said Mr Beecroft. 'I have no more questions.'

'Mr Mountfield,' said the Judge. 'Your turn to cross-examine.'

'Thank you, My Lord. Officer, is Dr Jayasuriya a man of hitherto good character?'

'Yes, he has no convictions recorded against him in the UK or Sri Lanka.'

'And it goes beyond that, does it not?' said Mr Mountfield. 'He is highly regarded by the University of Leeds for his work there, is he not?'

'Yes.'

'Which included many hours working as a demonstrator in anatomy?'

'Yes.'

'Which involved dissecting the human body?'

'Yes.'

'Those bodies or cadavers would come from the city's morgue?'

'Yes.'

'Bodies of people who, in their Wills, had said that their bodies could be used for medical research?'

'Yes.'

'Also bodies of unknown people, known as John Doe or Jane Doe, by that I mean bodies of people who were unidentified or claimed by their relatives?'

'Yes.'

'Did you discover that cadavers first go to the Dental School's oral biology lab before moving on to the biology lab for medical students?'

'Yes.'

'What enquiries did you make in Sri Lanka?'

'Detective Jane Rowley made enquiries there.'

'With what result?'

'That the accused had sought out Fathima because she was his daughter and arranged for her to come to the UK as his au pair.'

'The accused had told you that Fathima had returned to Sri Lanka, had he not?'

'Yes. There was no trace of her ever returning to Sri Lanka. If she had flown home, her name would have been recorded on an airline's passenger list. Furthermore, the accused did not come up with any explanation, during questioning, which justified asking for an adjournment to make further enquiries in Sri Lanka.'

'But you could have sought an adjournment?'

'We could, but we didn't as we were given no explanation for the bones. Also, there is a cost aspect. The decision was taken that in the absence of any evidence that she returned, we would not delay the trial for weeks whilst we went to Sri Lanka.

'If, as he should have done, the accused had given an explanation for the bones in interview or in his defence statement, we would have followed it up. To this day, he has given no such explanation.'

'Thank you, no more questions.'

'Any re-examination, Mr Beecroft?' asked the Judge.

'No, My Lord. That, My Lord, members of the jury, is the case for the prosecution,' said Beecroft.

Mountfield stood and said, 'My Lord, I have a submission to make which would be best done in the absence of the jury.'

'Very well,' said the judge, 'members of the jury, matters of law are for me. Would you retire for a short time whilst I hear Mr Mountfield?'

The jury retired.

'My Lord,' said Mountfield. 'I have a submission of no case to answer.'

'Yes,' said the Judge. 'Please go ahead.'

'My Lord, may it please you, there is no definite and reliable evidence that Fathima Mylvaganam is not alive. There is no proof that the bones found at Doctor Jayasuriya's house are hers. He is a demonstrator in anatomy. Who knows whose they are?'

'But why, Mr Mountfield, were they hidden?' asked the Judge.

'My Lord, I agree that is a difficulty I have, but it is not definitive of the issue.'

'But,' said the Judge. 'The girl disappears. She never returned to Sri Lanka even though, according to your client, that is where she said she was going.'

'No, Mr Mountfield, I am satisfied there is a case to answer.'

'If your Lordship pleases.'

'We'll adjourn now. We'll hear the case for the defence tomorrow morning.'

With that, the Judge withdrew.

Turnbull and Jasper went to the Jacob's Well for a drink. There were not many customers as it was mid-afternoon, so they took a seat at their usual table.

'What do you think?' asked Jasper.

'Well,' replied Turnbull. 'We'll soon find out. He has something up his sleeve. We should get ready to make enquiries.'

Chapter 23

Turnbull and Jasper arrived at Court the following morning. The jury had not yet come in; they were always brought in at the last moment to ensure that they didn't hear banter amongst Counsel's benches.

'Silence, all rise,' shouted the Court Clerk.

The Judge came in, followed by his clerk who sat further along the Judge's bench. The jury then filed in and sat in their usual places in the jury box.

'Yes, Mr Mountfield?' said the Judge.

'My Lord, before I call Chaminda Jayasuriya to give evidence in his own defence, may I just advise the members of the jury that there is no appropriate sacred text upon which to take an oath. Therefore, Doctor Jayasuriya will make the declaration in the prescribed manner.

'I now call Chaminda Jayasuriya to give evidence in his own defence.'

Accompanied by a prison officer, Doctor Jayasuriya came out of the dock. He looked very smart in a single-breasted grey suit, white shirt and black tie. His hair was immaculate, cut short and greying at the sides. He was handed a sheet of paper and requested to make his declaration.

'In accordance with the Buddhist precept of truthful speech and mindful of the consequences of false speech, I, Chaminda Jayasuriya, do solemnly, sincerely and truly declare and affirm that I will tell the whole truth and nothing but the truth.'

'What is your full name?' asked Mr Mountfield.

'Chaminda Jayasuriya.'

'And your occupation?'

'I am a lecturer in medicine at the University of Leeds, which appointment encompasses being a demonstrator in anatomy.'

'Where did you qualify?'

'In Sri Lanka, with a first class honours degree from the University of Ceylon. I practised in Sri Lanka for two years before coming to the UK.'

'How did you come to be in the UK?'

'I won a Commonwealth Scholarship to Durham University. After four years there, I came to Leeds University to take up my present position.'

'Do you have family?'

'Yes, my wife Tanoo and my ten-year-old son, Venkat.'

'Doctor Jayasuriya, did you murder Fathima Mylvaganam?'

'No. I am a doctor. My profession involves saving life, not taking it away.'

'Tell the jury about Fathima.'

'She came to the UK to be our au pair girl to look after our son, Venkat.'

'Did you know her before she came?'

'I knew of her. I am her father and arranged, through an agency in Sri Lanka which provides Sri Lankan au pairs to Sri Lankan citizens in the UK, for her to come here. She didn't know that I am her father, nor did my wife. I wanted to see how she had grown up.'

'How did you and she get on?'

'Very well, she was very industrious and respectful. She helped with the housework and looked after Venkat.'

'Were you ever intending to tell her that you were her father?'

'Yes, I was waiting for the appropriate moment.'

'Does your wife work?'

'Not at the moment but she did. She worked at a garden centre near Otley. She was the manager there. She worked long hours, hence the need for an au pair to look after Venkat.'

'How did Fathima get on with your son?'

'Very well. Venkat liked her a lot. During the summer holidays, I would give her money to take him on trips. They went all over on the bus.'

'Was she happy living with your family?'

'Yes, very happy. She was always smiling and anxious to help.'

'How long did she remain with you?'

'About six months. She intended to stay for one year or so, but she got a letter from her mother saying that she was ill and asking her to return home. We quite understood and offered to help in any way we could.'

'What happened to the letter?'

'I assume she took it with her. I never actually saw it. She said she had an open return airline ticket and could use that. I gave her a hundred pounds. She arranged her own transport. I had nothing to do with it. She said she was leaving the following morning without any fuss.

'I said I understood. I said goodbye to her in the morning before I went to work. She kissed me on the cheek and thanked me for all we had done for her. When I came home that night, she had gone. She never learnt that I'm her father as far as I'm aware, but I can't say for sure.'

'Doctor Jayasuriya, from your house, your garden and your laboratory at work, have been recovered a human skeleton. Whose skeleton is that?'

'I brought it in a trunk from Sri Lanka.'

Turnbull and Jasper heard the whole Court gasp. There were shouts from the public gallery and then there was a sudden silence whilst those in Court took in what he had just said. The Judge intervened.

'Mr Mountfield,' Mr Mountfield stood. 'Your client was cautioned before he was interviewed and warned that if he relied on, in Court, something he did not mention when questioned, that could harm his defence.'

'Yes, My Lord.'

'And his solicitor indicated then and there that he had explained the warning to his client. And yet, in interview, he never raised this explanation.'

'Yes, My Lord.'

'And then, when the time came to put in a defence statement, he made no mention of it either.'

'No, My Lord.'

'I cannot prevent him from giving this explanation, as long as both you and he understand that raising this defence for the first time in his evidence, must bring with it a strong warning in my summing up that the lateness of this disclosure may harm, i.e. made less credible, his defence.'

'My Lord, I quite understand.'

'Very well, carry on.'

'You were explaining, Doctor Jayasuriya, that you brought the skeleton with you from Sri Lanka.'

'Yes, each academic year, I was given a whole corpse to dissect. Before it was released to me, it would have been immersed in formalin and been injected with formalin into the deeper veins. The body would then be dissected in stages, by students, using scalpels. The skin, tissue and muscles which had been removed would be disposed of.

'At the end of the year, it would normally be sent for burial. However, when I got the job in the UK, I asked permission to bring the remains with me to the UK. By then, it was purely a skeleton as all the human tissue had been dissected and sent to the sluice. The skeleton, of course, was non-degradable.'

'So, you had an entire skeleton?'

'Yes, except for the teeth.'

'Why no teeth?'

'The corpse, before it came to me, had been at the dental department where they had extracted the teeth during their teaching sessions.'

'Also missing from the skeleton were the ribs. Why was that?'

'I must have misplaced them.'

'Why secrete the bones in the garden behind your garage, in plant pots, a holdall, in a container in your house and in your laboratory?'

'I wasn't secreting them, I knew where they were. I didn't want Venkat to find a human skeleton in the house. He was only ten years old. It would have frightened him. We don't have much storage space in the house, what with clothes. et cetera, so I spread parts of the skeleton around in the places where the police found them. I am, I accept, a bit, what's the word? Um, eccentric, but so is anyone who cuts up bodies.'

'Why were the bones so clean?'

'Well, as I said before, I had the skeleton for over a year. The remaining skeleton is a perfect example of how the body's skeleton is comprised, how all the pieces fit together. It's a marvel of nature.'

There were gasps and murmurs from the public gallery as this part of his evidence was taken on board.

'Why did you not give this explanation to the police?'

'I was advised not to by my solicitor.'

'But you knew that by not telling this to the police, it could make your evidence less credible, did you not?'

'Yes, but as the English saying goes, why keep a dog and bark yourself.'

There was laughter from the public gallery. Turnbull could see that the members of the press were having a field day.

'In saying that, I mean no disrespect to my solicitor, Mr Hodson, but I took his advice.'

'My Lord, is that a convenient moment to adjourn?' Mountfield asked the Judge.

'Yes, Mr Mountfield. Members of the jury, remember, no talking and I advise you not to read any newspapers or listen to or watch the news on television, from now on.'

'All rise,' instructed the Court Clerk.

The Court rose, Counsel bowed and the jury and the Judge withdrew to their respective rooms.

Turnbull turned to Jasper, 'I wasn't expecting that.'

'Nor was I,' said Jasper. 'But it's clever. It fits in with his defence that Fathima's still alive.'

'Let's go back to headquarters and discuss it with the team.'

* * *

At 6:00 p.m., Turnbull held a meeting in the boardroom at Bradford headquarters. Present were Bob Illingworth, who was in charge of the Murder Squad, Roberts and Jane Rowley together with Myles Gibson from the Crown Prosecution Service and, of course, Turnbull and Jasper.

'You bat first,' said Illingworth to Turnbull.

'Well, sir, we have been, to use an old-fashioned word, ambushed. The whole purpose of the rules set out in the Police and Criminal Evidence Act is to stop this happening, i.e. us being taken by surprise. I expect the defence will close their case in the morning and we either bat on as we are, or we are forced into asking for an adjournment to call evidence in rebuttal, if such evidence exists.'

'I agree,' said Illingworth. 'The Judge can't prevent him giving this evidence, but we are not immediately capable of rebutting it.'

'Well,' said Jasper. 'If I may. Would not asking for an adjournment give his evidence more credibility? It's so fanciful. Yet, if we start wanting time to rebut it, the jury may think there's genuinely something to rebut.'

'I agree,' said Myles Gibson. 'If we go down that route, it will mean sending someone to Sri Lanka to take statements and bring any witnesses back to the UK. That's to say, any witnesses we find who deal with this topic. And that could take weeks and would cost a fortune. I'm not sure my boss would be prepared to spend that sort of money.'

'Let's see what Beecroft and Oldroyd say,' said Illingworth. 'Have you spoken to them, Myles?'

'No, no chance in the hubbub. They said to me, "Let's meet at nine thirty tomorrow morning to discuss it".'

'Okay,' said Illingworth. 'For the moment, we'll stand fast and do nothing. Treat the explanation with the contempt it deserves. I mean, hiding bones in a plant pot, I ask you?'

'Fair enough, boss,' said Turnbull. 'Let's leave it 'til tomorrow.'

With that, they all gathered up their notes and went their separate ways.

Chapter 24

The following morning, Turnbull and Jasper met Counsel and Myles Gibson in a conference room at Bradford Crown Court.

Beecroft began the discussion by asking Turnbull what he thought.

'I suppose we should have seen it coming with him being a demonstrator in anatomy. We discussed the situation yesterday evening and the strengths of our case remain the unlikelihood of his explanation and the absence of any return flight.

'Rest assured, the accused has contacts in Sri Lanka. If the girl had returned, they would have produced her and this prosecution would never have taken place. Our enquiries, via her stepfather, show she never returned.

'So, we feel that seeking an adjournment to investigate, almost adds credence to his explanation. There is also the cost aspect of sending a man to Sri Lanka and bringing back witnesses from the University of Colombo.

'All in all, we think we carry on.'

'Well,' said Beecroft, 'that makes life easier. Oldroyd and I had come to much the same conclusion. Also, the jury will be told by the Judge that the credibility of this hair-brained defence is damaged by the failure to disclose it at the proper time. So, we bat on. See you in Court.'

With that, Beecroft and Oldroyd returned to their Robing Room.

* * *

At 10:30 a.m., the trial resumed. The accused entered the witness box.

'That concludes my examination of this witness,' said Mountfield.

Beecroft then stood to cross-examine.

'Do you make a habit of putting bones in plant pots, Doctor Jayasuriya?'

'No.'

'Have you ever, in your professional life, done it before?'

'No.'

'Why not put them all in a suitcase, for example, in your loft along with the holdall?'

'Yes, I suppose I could have done that.'

'Let's go back to Sri Lanka and this body. Whose was it?'

'I don't know.'

'But it was the body of a young girl. Surely she had a family?'

'I don't know. I was given the body for dissection.'

'Who by?'

'The supervisor of the morgue.'

'Did you have to sign for it?'

'Yes, I think so.'

'Do you have any documentation from the university to substantiate what you say?'

'No, it will be in Sri Lanka.'

'Did you ask anyone for permission to help yourself to this skeleton?'

'No, I didn't need to.'

'Did anyone help you to load it into a trunk?'

'No, by then it was a skeleton, so it wasn't heavy. It was on a skeleton stand, hanging from a hook on the stand.'

'So, you had no idea who it was?'

'No. It was a Jane Doe as you British call it. Never claimed by anyone as a relative.'

'And is it just a coincidence that it corresponds with the height and age of Fathima Mylvaganam?'

'I don't know if it does.'

Mountfield rose to object. 'My Lord, whether or not it corresponds with the height and age of Fathima Mylvaganam is a matter for the jury to decide in the light of Professor Talbot's evidence in cross-examination.'

'I agree,' said the Judge.

Mr Beecroft bowed and said, 'If your Lordship pleases.' He then continued.

'Did you declare the skeleton at Customs?'

'No, it wasn't necessary. It was just part of my luggage.'

'How, in the absence of human tissue, was the skeleton held together?'

'By metal pins and brackets or by wire and springs. I can't remember which. Those are the common ways of keeping a skeleton intact.'

'But no pins, brackets wire or springs were recovered. How do you explain that?'

'When I had finished using it for demonstration, I disassembled it and threw everything except the bones away.'

'Did not the pins, brackets, wires or springs leave marks on the skeleton?'

'I don't think so.'

'Surely wires would need holes in the skeleton for the wires to be put through?'

'I don't know.'

'And surely if you were keeping it, you would also keep the equipment necessary to hold it together?'

'I didn't think of that.'

'You see, no suggestion was made to Professor Talbot, by defence Counsel, that there were holes in the bones through which the wires were threaded to hold the skeleton together.'

'I don't remember any holes.'

'Did your wife know about the bones secreted in plant pots and elsewhere?'

'No.'

'She could have got the shock of her life if she'd discovered them when she was watering the plants. Didn't you think about that possibility?'

'No, because I look after the plants and the garden, not her.'

'Surely, she could have come across the bones you had secreted in the container in the kitchen as that is her province, not yours?'

'She knows I am eccentric. She would just think it was me being odd. If I had wanted to dispose of the bones, I could easily have dumped them on Baildon Moors.'

'Is it not true that the reason the ribs are missing, is because some were damaged when you stabbed Fathima with a knife?'

'Why would I stab her? I was very fond of her. She's my daughter for God's sake. We never disagreed about anything.'

'Do you still have family in Sri Lanka?'

'Yes, two brothers and a sister. All three are married.'

'Your case is that Fathima is still alive so have you had your family look for her in Sri Lanka.'

'Yes.'

'Without success?'

'They have not found her.'

'Do you know whether the police in Sri Lanka have been asked to search for her?'

'I assume so. I could do nothing. I have been in custody.'

'But surely if she had been found, you would have heard?'

Mr Mountfield stood. 'My Lord, I object to this line of questioning. The answer has to be hearsay. The defendant can have no knowledge of such matters other than by hearsay.'

The Judge addressed Mr Beecroft. 'That is right, is it not, Mr Beecroft?'

'My Lord, I will move on,' replied Beecroft.

Not before the point is made, thought Turnbull.

'You distributed the body not only in your house, in the garden behind your garage but also at your laboratory in a coffee jar, a steel tray, a beaker and in your desk drawer. Why not all in one place?'

'I can't remember, but they could easily be traced to me, as they have been.'

'The truth is, Doctor Jayasuriya, that this defence is a smokescreen to hide the fact that you murdered this girl and sought to hide her body.'

'That is not true.'

'You have lived a lie, have you not, never telling your wife that Fathima was your daughter?'

'That is true.'

'And you brought her here purely to satisfy your curiosity, did you not?'

'That is not true.'

'You played with her and then you murdered her.'

'That is not true.'

Mr Beecroft sat down.

'Have you any re-examination, Mr Mountfield?' asked the Judge.

'One question, if I may. Have you ever killed anyone, Doctor Jayasuriya?'

'No. Patients have died under my care, but I would never kill anyone. I am a doctor.'

'Thank you, Doctor Jayasuriya, you may return to the dock. That, My Lord, is the case for the defence,' said Mountfield.

'Thank you, Mr Mountfield; we will adjourn until ten thirty tomorrow morning. Members of the jury, remember my warning, no talking.'

'All rise,' called the Court Clerk.

Everyone stood, Counsel bowed and the Judge and jury withdrew.

'Let's go for a pint,' said Turnbull to Jasper.

'Good idea, shall I ring Roberts and Rowley and tell them to meet us at the pub, that's if you're buying?'

'Okay,' replied Turnbull as they made their way out of the courtroom.

Chapter 25

The following morning at 10:30, the Court reassembled.

The Judge addressed the jury.

'The timetable now is that you will hear speeches. Firstly, from Mr Beecroft for the Crown and then from Mr Mountfield for the defence. After that, I will sum up the case to you.

'I expect you will be going out to consider your verdict at some point tomorrow morning.

'Yes, Mr Beecroft.'

Beecroft stood to address the jury, leaning on the small table which was on top of Counsel's benches. Only Queen's Counsel, by tradition, are allowed to use such a table.

'May it please your Lordship, members of the jury,' said Beecroft. 'The defence raised in this case is pure fantasy. Surely, if Fathima was still alive, the agency through which Doctor Jayasuriya had booked her, would have traced her; she would have got in touch with the Jayasuriyas to say where she was. She could then have confirmed to Missing Persons, in the UK, that she was alive and well and this trial would never have taken place.

'Her mother could easily have been traced by the agency and she could have confirmed that she has been ill and that her daughter returned home to see her and look after her.

'Her stepfather, who is alive and well and with whom she lived before she came to the UK, could have got in touch with the UK authorities to say she is alive and well.

'Remember, Doctor Jayasuriya has a very competent solicitor in Mr Richard Hodson who has sat in Court throughout. His job is to prepare the defence case.

'Yet, total silence. So, presumably, having disappeared here, she has disappeared in Sri Lanka also. It is fantasy.

'And, how did she get there? She didn't fly. That much is clear from the uncontested evidence of the airlines' co-ordinator. If she had flown back on an open return ticket, we would surely have found that out. In this modern technological world, you can't move without it being recorded.

'So, nothing from Sri Lanka and nothing from the airlines. But, lo and behold, there is found at Doctor Jayasuriya's house, a skeleton of precisely the dimensions of the missing girl. What an unfortunate coincidence for Doctor Jayasuriya.

'His explanation? It is the skeleton he brought from Sri Lanka for research purposes and demonstration to his students. Surely there are skeletons available in the UK for demonstration, just as there are in Sri Lanka, so why bring his own skeleton?

'And what does he do with this skeleton, which is no doubt precious to him? After all the trouble he took to bring it from Sri Lanka, he disassembles it and secretes bits in different places around the house, in his garden and in his laboratory at the University of Leeds.

'And then he loses certain parts of the skeleton, the ribs. Is it another coincidence that, if stabbed, this victim's ribs would, in all probability, show nicks in the bone which the knife caught on its way to the heart? Just look at the places he put his precious skeleton. In a hole dug in the garden behind the garage; in plant pots in the hallway. It is all fantasy.

'And why was this defence not raised in interviews with the police or in his defence statement? The reason is the defence knew we would check it out and prove it to be fantasy.

'And if this skeleton had been held together by wires, there would be holes visible to Professor Talbot. Yet there were none.

'The truth, ladies and gentlemen of the jury, is that Doctor Jayasuriya, for reasons known maybe only to himself and the victim, murdered Fathima Mylvaganam, his daughter, whose existence he never disclosed to his wife. We don't know for sure how or why he murdered her. All we have to prove is that he did it.

'My Lord will tell you that motive is not an ingredient of the offence which the Crown has to prove. What we must prove is that with intent either to kill or cause grievous bodily harm, he took this young girl's life. And that we have done.

'Your only possible verdict is one of guilty of murder.'

Beecroft sat down.

The Judge addressed Mr Mountfield. 'Are you ready to address the jury, Mr Mountfield?'

'Yes, My Lord, perhaps at 2:00 p.m. so that the members of the jury may have a break.'

'Certainly. Members of the jury, please return to Court at 2:00 p.m.'

'All rise,' said the Court Clerk and the Judge and jury withdrew.

'Let's go for some lunch, Dave,' said Turnbull. 'We'll go to that little Italian restaurant around the corner. Juries don't tend to go there. I'll treat you.'

'You're on, thanks,' said Jasper.

Turnbull and Jasper walked out of Court into the Bradford sunshine and headed for the restaurant. They were shown to a table where they sat and, after a brief look at the menu, ordered spaghetti vongole and a couple of glasses of Pinot Grigio.

'I thought Beecroft's speech was good,' said Turnbull. 'Short and to the point and laying bare the farcical nature of the defence.'

'I agree,' said Jasper. 'But Mountfield's clever and he's

capable of pulling a rabbit out of a hat. Juries are also extremely fickle and are capable of producing verdicts which in no way reflect the weight of the evidence.'

'Well,' said Turnbull. 'There's nothing more we can do now. We decided not to seek an adjournment. It's now in the lap of the Gods and twelve good men and true.'

'Hold on,' said Jasper. 'Most of the jurors are women.'

'Well, you know what I mean,' said Turnbull. 'In any case, women on the whole are wiser than men.'

'So you say. Another glass of Pinot?'

'Why not?'

Chapter 26

The Court reassembled.

Mountfield stood to address the jury.

'May it please your Lordship, members of the jury, a fantasy my Learned Friend calls the defence.

'Is it a fantasy that Doctor Jayasuriya is a demonstrator in anatomy? Is it a fantasy that in that capacity, he has access to corpses? Is it a fantasy that there is no scientific evidence that the skeleton is that of Fathima Mylvaganam?

'The prosecution case, I will suggest to you, is speculation. Had there been teeth, the situation may have been different, but there weren't. Had there been a sign of damage such as would most often be caused by a knife; the situation may have been different. But there wasn't.

'Had there been signs of blunt impact by a hard object to the skull, the situation may have been different, but there wasn't. Had flesh or human tissue adhered to the bones, the situation may have been different.

'But none of these considerations applied. So, the Crown is left having to ask you to speculate that the skeleton is that of Fathima Mylvaganam.

'There is no way of knowing how old the bones are which were found at Doctor Jayasuriya's house. And if they were the bones of Fathima, would he have kept them in his house? Surely he would have dumped them in the Leeds Liverpool canal at nearby Apperley Bridge, or in the river Wharfe at Ilkley, or on Baildon Moors. Why keep them close to home?

'No, the defence is not fantasy. However, the prosecution is speculation, asking you to fill in the gaps.

'There is no way you can be sure that this skeleton was that of Fathima Mylvaganam. The Crown is asking you to add two and two to make five. Their case is seriously depleted.

'And what's more, the Crown seems to have forgotten where the burden of proof lies. It is for the Crown to prove Doctor Jayasuriya's guilt, not for the defence to prove he is innocent.

'The Crown has at its disposal huge assets. The defendant is legally aided. Why could not the Crown call evidence from Sri Lanka to discredit the defence?

'Yet, nothing. All they have is the bones and those bones are not ageable beyond saying they are of a teenage girl who could have died at any time.

'No, the Crown cannot, on this evidence, have made you sure of guilt and the only safe verdict in this case is one of not guilty.'

'Thank you, Mr Mountfield,' said the Judge.

Chapter 27

The Judge addressed the jury.

'Members of the jury, this is indeed an unusual case because the defence here is that there has been no murder. The alleged victim is, so far as the defence is concerned, still alive.

'In deciding whether the prosecution has proved that there has indeed been a murder, you and I have very different functions. I am the judge of the law and procedure. I give rulings on matters of law, but you are the sole judges of the facts. It is for you to decide whether Fathima Mylvaganam was murdered and, if so, by this defendant.

'And, in making that decision, you must bear in mind this fundamental principle. Anyone charged with a criminal offence in this country, is presumed to be innocent until proved guilty and it follows that where the prosecution bring a charge, they must prove it on the whole of the evidence, which includes the evidence called on behalf of the defence.

'Sometimes, the defence evidence weakens or destroys the prosecution case and explains away evidence which otherwise has not been explained. Whether that applies here, to the evidence of Doctor Jayasuriya, is a matter entirely for you.

'The prosecution say the defence case is pure fantasy. The defence say Doctor Jayasuriya's evidence was perfectly credible and they do not have to prove anything. The purpose of Doctor Jayasuriya's evidence was in order to cast doubt on the prosecution case, but also to persuade you that Doctor Jayasuriya is not a murderer.

'The standard which the prosecution must attain before you could convict Doctor Jayasuriya is a high one. They must make each and every one of you sure of guilt.

'So, the question which you must ask yourselves, when you retire, is *am I sure upon a calm, quiet, objective view of all the evidence, putting aside all question of sympathy or bias, that Doctor Jayasuriya is guilty?*

'If you are sure, you must convict. If you are less than sure, you must acquit.

'Let me turn to the law of murder. Murder is the unlawful killing of another with the intention either to kill or to cause grievous bodily harm, i.e. really serious injury.

'The Crown says that they do not know how Fathima was murdered, nor do they know why she was murdered.

'However, motive is not an ingredient of the offence of murder. In other words, the prosecution do not have to prove that Doctor Jayasuriya had a reason for murdering her, merely that he did.

'Doctor Jayasuriya's defence is that he never murdered Fathima. He had no reason to. He was very fond of her. He disclosed for the first time in evidence that she is, or was, his daughter. She left prematurely because she said her mother was ill. He doesn't know whether that is true or false, but that is the reason she gave.

'You know that the accused, Doctor Jayasuriya, is a man of good character. He qualified as a doctor in Sri Lanka with, he says, first class honours, and came to this country to the University of Leeds as a lecturer and demonstrator in anatomy. You are entitled to take his hitherto unblemished character into account in two ways.

'Firstly, say the defence, he is unlikely, as a doctor, to commit a brutal murder. Secondly, his good character is relevant to his credibility as a witness. You are more likely, it is said, to place reliance on the word of a person of good character than you are upon the word of a man who has shown, in the past, to be dishonest.

'Of course, good character cannot fight facts; otherwise a person of good character would never be convicted of anything.

'Before each interview, the defendant was cautioned. He was told: *you do not have to say anything when questioned, but it may harm your defence if you do not mention, when questioned, something which you later rely on in Court.*

'Similarly, the rules dictate that a defendant must put in a defence statement, after being served with the witness statements, upon which the prosecution rely. A failure to set out in detail his case in relation to those matters in respect of which he takes issue, can also be held against him.

'Well, Doctor Jayasuriya went into the witness box and did precisely that. He gave an explanation for the bones found at his house and at his laboratory. The purpose of the rule is to prevent an ambush, the late raising of a defence which takes the prosecution by surprise and without enough time to check it out. That is exactly what has happened. And the defence solicitor knew this would happen when he advised his client to *no comment.*

'The extent to which you hold these deliberate failures into account in assessing Doctor Jayasuriya's credibility, is a matter for you to decide.

'We will adjourn now until ten thirty tomorrow morning. Remember my warnings.'

Turnbull and Jasper went back to their office. They had other cases on the boil which had been neglected and which required their attention, so now was the time to catch up.

Chapter 28

The following morning, the Judge continued with his summing up.

'I now turn to remind you of the salient parts of the evidence. I will not repeat everything, but if I omit to mention something you regard as important, give that evidence such attention as you see fit. My summary of the facts is just that, a summary.

'There will be no more evidence. So, when you retire, you cannot send me a question which cannot be answered by the evidence already given. There is no evidence from Sri Lanka. Either side could have called evidence, but decided not to. Do not speculate about what that evidence could have, or would have, been.

'The story begins, does it not, with the arrival of Fathima Mylvaganam as an au pair girl at the household of Doctor Jayasuriya and his wife, Tanoo. She was there to help in the house and look after ten-year-old Venkat, their son. Tanoo worked and so needed help. From then on, Doctor Jayasuriya was in *loco parentis* of this young girl who was in her late teens. She also, it transpires, is, or was, his daughter. He traced her and arranged for her to come here as an au pair.

'Fathima would visit the next-door neighbours, John and Liz Campbell, with Venkat. The Campbell's have a son, Henry, of similar age. The two boys would play cricket on the Campbell's lawn whilst Fathima would chat with Mrs Campbell and occasionally help her in the house. Fathima and Liz Campbell became quite friendly.

'After a period of months, however, the Campbells no longer saw Fathima. They sought an explanation from Doctor

Jayasuriya.

'They were told, by Doctor Jayasuriya, that the girl had returned to Sri Lanka, on an open ticket, because her mother was ill. The Campbells were not happy with this explanation as Fathima had never mentioned her mother, or her illness, to them nor, it seems, did she mention it to her English teacher or her boyfriend, whom she had stood up without explanation.

'After several more weeks, the Campbells decided, reluctantly, to report Fathima as a missing person. Their departmental enquiries revealed no sign of Fathima flying back to Sri Lanka. And so, Missing Persons reported what they thought was her disappearance to the Murder Squad and to DCI James Turnbull. His team's enquiries also came to nought.

'So they went to see Doctor and Mrs Jayasuriya to ask them about Fathima's disappearance. Doctor Jayasuriya repeated that Fathima had flown back to Sri Lanka because her mother was ill. DCI Turnbull was not satisfied. A search of Fathima's bedroom revealed two hundred pounds in twenty pound notes under the mattress.

'The police then decided to obtain a search warrant of Doctor Jayasuriya's house, grounds and workplace and an order for disclosure of her bank account. Buried in the garden, behind the garage, they found human bones. Other human bones were found in three plant pots in the hallway; in a container in the kitchen and in a holdall in the loft.

'Bones were also recovered from Doctor Jayasuriya's laboratory and office at the University of Leeds.

'Her bank account was in credit to the tune of two thousand pounds. That money had never been touched.

'When asked for an explanation, in interview, Doctor Jayasuriya made no comment. And that remained his position until he gave evidence in this, his trial.

'His explanation for the bones, which made an almost complete skeleton save for some ribs and all the teeth, is that the corpse is a skeleton he brought from Sri Lanka in order to use it in demonstrations for students in anatomy classes.

'The Crown, we know, rely principally on three pieces of evidence.

'Firstly, the girl had an open return ticket which was never used. It is impossible, according to the Emirates official, for her to have used it without its use being recorded. She would have had to have booked a seat, presented her ticket at the check-in desk, received a boarding card, shown that at the gate and then to cabin staff on the plane. For none of this to happen and yet Fathima flying back to Sri Lanka is impossible.

'Secondly, the bones found correspond with what Fathima's bones would have looked like. Professor Talbot was never asked in cross-examination, which he should have been, if holes were found in the bones consistent with the use of wires to hold the skeleton together. If he had found such holes, no doubt he would have told us.

'Thirdly, the Crown say the bones were hidden and the obvious reason for that is that she had been murdered.

'Doctor Jayasuriya says: "Not so. I was allocated a corpse in Sri Lanka for my work with students as a demonstrator in anatomy. The bones found were those from that skeleton. The reason they were so clean is that all tissue had been used in dissection in Sri Lanka. The ageing of the bones is inevitably an approximation. There is nothing inconsistent with the bones being those of my skeleton brought from Sri Lanka. I put them where they were found so that Venkat would not be frightened by the sight of a skeleton. If I wanted to dispose of them completely, I could easily have done so. Why keep them so close to home?"

'The rest of the evidence has been given so recently that I don't think it necessary to remind you any more of it.

'You must decide whether you are sure this girl was murdered by Doctor Jayasuria and that the skeleton recovered is hers and not that of a skeleton brought from Sri Lanka by Doctor Jayasuriya.

'You may have heard that, in certain circumstances, I can accept from you a verdict which is not the verdict of you all. Those circumstances have not as yet arisen. So, when you retire, you must strive to reach a verdict upon which you are all agreed. If a time arises when I can accept from you a verdict which is not the verdict of you all, I will call you back into Court to give you a further direction.

'When the Jury Bailiffs have been sworn, will you please retire to consider your verdict? If you have any issue upon which I can be of assistance, write it down, give it to your usher and I will give you such assistance as I can. I repeat, however, that there will be no more evidence.

'So, if you send me a question, please remember that if evidence has not been given on the topic you are asking about, all I can do is remind you of what has been said in evidence in the trial.

'Please appoint one of your number as your foreman who will chair your deliberations and, in due course, let the Court know your verdict.'

The Jury Bailiffs were then sworn to look after the jury during their retirement. They would remain outside the jury room and only enter when invited to do so by the jury.

The jury then withdrew.

The time was two minutes past noon.

'Get the team together, Dave,' said Turnbull. 'I'm buying lunch at the Indian up the road.'

With that, they left the Court and headed for the restaurant. They ordered Kingfisher beers and perused the menu whilst they waited for Roberts and Rowley to arrive. A huge plate of poppadoms arrived, together with a pickle tray, just as Roberts and Rowley walked in.

'Hi boss,' they said, almost in unison.

'Thanks for this,' said Roberts.

'That's okay,' said Turnbull. 'Let's order.'

'That summing up was a bit lacklustre,' observed Jasper.

'I don't know,' said Turnbull. 'The days of pro-pros summings up are over. It was balanced, if a bit dull.

'I remember when Judges used to have a bit more oomph, with a good sense of humour. I remember Judge Geoffrey Baker QC trying an appeal by Jake Mangleworsel, the Huddersfield eccentric. He was charged with impersonating a police officer. He rode around Huddersfield on a motor scooter with E C I L O P emblazoned on his back. That's police spelt backwards.

'God only knows how the magistrates had convicted him on that evidence, but they had. Mangleworsel appealed to the Crown Court. Judge Geoffrey Baker entered Court in his full bottomed wig, tights, patent leather shoes with buckles and, of course, his robes. He bowed to Counsel. Mangleworsel then flounced into Court dressed as a court jester. He did a twirl and made an extravagant bow to the Judge before entering the dock. The Judge said nothing.

'After a time, Mangleworsel looked vexed that the Judge had made no comment about his extravagant dress, so he stood at an appropriate moment and said to the Judge: *Your eminence, you haven't made any comment about my attire. I am the Town Crier of Huddersfield and these pantaloons and my jacket with bells on, together with my three-cornered hat, are my official dress.*

'The Judge looked at him and said: *Don't think anything of it, Mr Mangleworsel, look what they make me wear* – and carried on as if nothing had happened.'

'Boss, I love your stories,' said Jane. 'I hope, when I'm your age, I have a lot of stories like yours.'

'Hey, not so much of the *when I'm your age*,' replied Turnbull as he helped himself to some more Rogan josh and rice. 'I still have a few years left in me.'

'Boss, how's cricket?' asked Roberts. 'We haven't heard you talking about it much.'

'Well,' said Turnbull as he took another sip of his beer. 'Yorkshire is strong and when Yorkshire's strong, England's strong. Captain Michael Vaughan is a Yorkshireman as is Matthew Hoggard, strike bowler, and Ryan Sidebottom. That's how it should be.'

'Who are they playing?' asked Roberts.

'India at The Oval in August,' replied Turnbull. 'I've taken leave so I can go.'

The group tucked in to an excellent Indian lunch and a few Kingfisher beers.

After a good meal, Roberts looked at his watch and said: 'Let's be off. It's two o'clock, we'd better get back to HQ, but thanks for lunch.'

'You're welcome,' said Turnbull as Roberts and Rowley got up from the table.

Turnbull paid the bill and he and Jasper went back to the Crown Court.

Chapter 29

The rest of the day passed slowly. Turnbull and Jasper sat in the Police Room reading the papers, waiting for the jury to return a verdict.

At 4:30 p.m. the Judge called the jury back into Court and sent them home until the following day.

* * *

At 10:30 the following morning, the jury was sent out again to continue with their deliberations.

Turnbull and Jasper were, by now, beginning to get a bit worried. The jury had been out for more than seven hours.

'Maybe it's just one or two standing out,' said Jasper. 'And when we get a majority direction from the Judge, they'll be back quickly.'

'I hope so,' said Turnbull. 'They could be hopelessly tied.'

'Let's hope not,' said Jasper.

At 2:00 p.m. the Judge sent for the jury.

The Court Clerk stood. 'My Lord, the jury has been deliberating for nine hours twenty minutes.'

'Thank you,' said the Judge. 'Members of the jury, sufficient time has now elapsed whereby I can accept from you a verdict which is not the verdict of you all. From now on I can accept a verdict on which at least ten of you are agreed. Ten to two, eleven to one, or a unanimous verdict, i.e. one on which you are all agreed.

'So, will you retire again and strive to reach a verdict upon which you are all agreed. If that is not possible, I can accept from you a verdict upon which at least ten of you are agreed.'

The jury left Court, looking particularly miserable. One woman was shaking her head.

At 4:30 p.m. the jury were sent home with instructions to reconvene at 10:30 the following morning.

The following morning, the Judge addressed Counsel in the absence of the jury.

'Mr Beecroft, Mr Mountfield, I am disposed to give the jury what you know as a Watson direction. Have you any observations to make on that?'

'No, My Lord,' said Counsel in turn.

'Thank you,' said the Judge. 'Jury back please.'

The members of the jury filed into Court.

'Members of the jury,' said the Judge. 'Each of you has taken an oath to return a verdict according to the evidence. No one must be false to that oath but you have a duty, not only as individuals but collectively, that is the strength of the jury system.

'Each of you takes into the jury box with you your individual experience and wisdom. Your task is to pool that experience and wisdom. You do that by giving your own views and listening to the views of others. There must necessarily be discussion, argument and give and take within the scope of your oath. That is the way in which agreement is reached.

'If, unhappily, ten of you cannot reach agreement, you must say so.

'Will you now retire once more to continue with your deliberations?'

* * *

James Turnbull and Dave Jasper went to the Police Room and read the papers.

'I can't think what's worrying them. To me, it's an open and shut case,' said Jasper.

'Maybe to you but, obviously, not to them. Various things stick out from the defence case. The bones were as clean as a whistle, which suggests a skeleton used for anatomy lessons. It's not possible to be certain the skeleton is Fathima's.

'And Jayasuriya is a demonstrator in anatomy and is of good character. I'm being the devil's advocate here, but I can see where the problems may lie.'

'Well, you may be right,' said Jasper. 'If they can't agree, do we ask for a re-trial? The CPS won't like that with all the expense.'

Just as they were talking, an usher knocked on the door. 'We have a verdict,' he said.

Turnbull and Jasper returned to their seats in Court, behind Myles Gibson.

There was a deathly hush.

The jury entered the Court and all sat looking rather po-faced not looking at the accused. Turnbull knew all the negative signs.

'All rise,' was the call as the Judge entered. He bowed and sat.

The Clerk stood to address the jury. 'Will the foreman please stand.'

Up stood a plump, middle-aged man with a moustache. Turnbull wondered whether he'd ever had to make a decision in his life before this.

'Mr Foreman, has the jury reached a verdict in respect of which at least ten of you are agreed?'

'Yes.'

There was a complete hush in Court.

'Do you find the defendant, Chaminda Jayasuriya, guilty or not guilty of murder?'

'Guilty.'

There was a mixture of moans and claps from the public gallery. The Judge waited for quiet.

Mr Beecroft stood and said to the Judge, 'As you know, the defendant is a man of good character. There are no other matters outstanding.' He sat.

Mr Mountfield stood, 'My Lord, as you know, the defendant has maintained his innocence of this crime throughout this trial and, in those circumstances, it would be inappropriate for me to address you in mitigation.'

'Thank you, Mr Mountfield. Stand up please,' he said to the defendant.

'You have been convicted of the callous murder of your seventeen-year-old daughter whose whole life was ahead of her. Why you did it, only you know.

'There is only one sentence the law permits and that is life imprisonment, which sentence I now pass.

'You will serve a minimum of twenty-five years in prison before you are eligible to apply for parole.

'Take the defendant down.'

'I'm innocent I tell you,' shouted Jayasuriya as he was led away. 'She's alive, I tell you, she's alive.'

Turnbull and Jasper greeted Beecroft and Oldroyd outside Court.

'That was a close run thing,' said Beecroft.

With that, all four left to go their separate ways.

Chapter 30

Tanoo collected Venkat and they went back to their home on Forest Hill completely dumbfounded. They tried to lead a normal life as best they could. Tanoo was ignored in the village. She felt like a leper. The trial had been the subject of enormous publicity in the local papers and on television. *How the jury could be unaffected by it all,* thought Tanoo: *God only knows.* She went to seek the solace of the monk at the temple which she and Chaminda used to attend occasionally, but that didn't help much. She was more worried about how Venkat would be received at school, but he never complained.

They had received advice that there was no appeal, so this was their life from now on, visiting Chaminda in prison.

One evening in late September, Tanoo was at home. There was a knock on the door. She wondered who could be calling on them at this hour. She thought it might be the press and was in two minds whether or not to answer it. She opened the front door and couldn't believe what she saw.

There stood Fathima, smiling, with her suitcase in hand.

'Can it be you?' she said. 'I don't believe this. Are you a ghost or are you really Fathima?'

'Of course I am,' she said and she stepped forward to kiss Tanoo on the cheek.

'Where is Chaminda?' she asked.

'He's in prison. Surely you know that.'

'No,' she gasped. 'And what are all the floorboards up for?'

'To search for your bones.'

'What? I don't understand.'

'Where have you been?'

'Well, I discovered that Chaminda is my father and I was so shocked, I didn't know what to do or think so I decided to go to a Buddhist retreat near Plymouth. I said my mother was ill cos I didn't think you'd let me go otherwise. So I got a lift into Baildon, then a train to Leeds and on to Plymouth. It's a direct line.'

'But haven't you seen the papers and television? Your father has been convicted of your murder on the basis of bones he had discarded from work. You know how eccentric he is. He had left them in odd places so that Venkat didn't find them. The police took them to be yours. He was tried and convicted and sentenced to life imprisonment.'

'I had no idea,' said Fathima. 'There are no papers or television at the retreat. Time there is spent in meditation and growing vegetables. One had no worldly possessions, no money, nothing. I stood it for a few months, but then I thought: *this is not for me, I should be with my family.* You are my family now, so I have come back.'

'Why did you leave your money under your mattress?' asked Tanoo.

'With all the stress, I forgot about it. I didn't need money at the retreat and I had enough for my fare. Don't you want me?'

'Of course we want you, but how do we get your father back? Oh, wait a minute. I have that policeman's card. He said to ring him any time. I think it's on the mantelpiece in the sitting room,' said Tanoo as she moved quickly to retrieve it.

'Yes, here it is. I'll ring him now and Richard Hodson, our solicitor.'

She rang the number. Turnbull answered quickly, 'DCI Turnbull.'

'Yes, Mr Turnbull, this is Tanoo Jayasuria. You said to ring you at any time. I didn't know what else to do.'

'Of course,' said Turnbull. 'How can I help you?'

'Well, Mr Turnbull, you won't believe this, but Fathima has just walked into the house, alive and well.'

'What?' he exclaimed.

'Yes, she's standing here in front of me, as alive as I am.'

'Well, blow my soul, I'll be right round.'

'Is Daddy coming home?' asked Venkat who had been standing in the doorway of his bedroom.

'Let's hope so, darling, let's hope so.'

Next she rang Richard Hodson and told him what had happened. He was as surprised as DCI Turnbull had been.

'We were thrown off the scent by Fathima saying she was going back to Sri Lanka because her mother was ill,' said Richard Hodson. 'Don't worry, Tanoo, I'll get Chaminda back as soon as ever possible.'

When the calls had finished, Tanoo and Fathima sat down. 'Shall we have a drink?' said Tanoo.

'Good idea,' said Fathima. 'A large glass of white wine please and tomorrow I'll get on to my Sri Lankan friends to come and help us put everything back in order. They're a talented lot. And I'll get Liz and John Campbell to come and help as well. After all, it was he who set this ball rolling.'

'Okay, that would be good, but I think your first priority is to ring Phillip Green. He has been very upset and worried about you.'

'Oh dear,' said Fathima. 'He is so lovely, I'm sorry I have upset him. Yes, of course, I will ring him in the morning. Perhaps he'll come and help too.

'Before that, I must ring my Dad, sorry stepfather, to put his mind at rest.'

He answered straight away and Fathima explained what had happened.

'I had been told you'd disappeared and that there had been a trial and your employer had murdered you. Oh God, I'm so happy to hear your voice, Fathima. I have been distraught. I was about to arrange your funeral over here. The bones that had been recovered were to be sent to me by the Home Office. How macabre.

'Well, I've got you back and that's all that matters. I love you so much, Fathima.'

'I love you too,' said Fathima.

Once the police confirmed that Fathima Mylvaganam was alive, the legal machinery sprang into motion. A bail application secured Chaminda Jayasuriya's release from prison, the Home Secretary herself having intervened. The Court of Appeal's (Criminal Division) hearing was expedited after the involvement of the Lord Chancellor. The case was listed in one week before the Lord Chief Justice and two senior Lord Justices of Appeal.

Mr Mountfield QC and Mr Blackstone appeared on behalf of the Appellant, Chaminda Jayasuriya, as they had done at the trial and the Crown was represented by Mr Beecroft QC and Mr Oldroyd, who also appeared in the trial. Also present was another QC who was there to represent the interests of the Home Office.

The press gallery was full, which was only to be expected as the pending hearing had featured heavily in the press.

The case was called on Chaminda Jayasuriya, and his wife, Tanoo, sat and watched from their seats at the back of the Court. He was identified and sat down.

'May it please your Lordships,' said Mountfield from the front row of Counsel's benches. 'I appear together with my learned friend, Mr Blackstone, on behalf of the Appellant, Doctor Chaminda Jayasuriya. The Crown, the Respondent in this appeal, is represented by my learned friends Mr Beecroft and Mr Oldroyd. We all appeared in the Court below. For reasons which will become obvious, The Home Office is presented by my learned friend Mr Batty.

'My Lords, this is a tragic case in which a gross miscarriage of justice has been avoided by luck rather than judgment.'

Turnbull, who sat in Court with Jasper, squirmed.

'On the thirteenth of September this year, Chaminda Jayasuriya was convicted of the murder of Fathima Mylvaganam. Doctor Jayasuriya was sentenced to life imprisonment, with a minimum term to be served of twenty-five years. He was three weeks into his sentence when the alleged victim of his murder, Fathima Mylvaganam, turned up at the Jayasuriyas' family home.

'She had told the Jayasuriyas that she was returning to Sri Lanka because her mother was ill. This was a lie and it has led to the injustice from which Doctor Jayasuriya suffered and still suffers. The excuse given for the lie was that she did not believe Doctor Jayasuriya would release her from her duties unless she gave a reason for leaving. She thought the reason she gave was both plausible and compelling.

'In fact, she never had any intention of returning to Sri Lanka. She intended to go to a Buddhist Retreat outside Plymouth. And that is where she went, by train from Leeds to Plymouth.

'The Retreat is what it says, a place cut off from the outside world with no radio, television or newspapers. Thus, Fathima had no idea that in her absence, in a glare of publicity, Doctor Jayasuriya had been arrested and tried for her murder, convicted and sentenced to life imprisonment.

'The reason Fathima left the Jayasuriyas' family home was that she discovered that Doctor Jayasuriya was her natural father, born of a relationship he had with her mother some eighteen years earlier, Her mother had then married and Fathima became part of her stepfather's family. When that marriage broke up, Fathima chose to remain with her stepfather and changed her name to Mylvaganam. Thereafter, she regarded her stepfather as her natural father.

'She came to England as an au pair to look after Doctor and Mrs Jayasuriya's ten-year-old son. She was very happy until she discovered from a birth certificate on Doctor Jayasuriya's desk that Doctor Jayasuriya was in fact her natural father.

'This caused considerable confusion in the poor girl's mind. She made the excuse that her mother was ill and had to return to Sri Lanka to look after her when, in fact, she left to go to the Buddhist Retreat to think about the implications of her discovery.

'Meanwhile, her disappearance was noticed by neighbours and was reported to the police who made extensive enquiries and eventually conducted a search of Doctor Jayasuriya's house, garden and place of work.

'They found human bones secreted in the garden, various places within the house and various places in his office and laboratory at the University of Leeds. These were identified by Professor Talbot as human bones and corresponded exactly with those of a seventeen-year-old girl.

'Thus, the police were convinced they had found the bones of Fathima. The fact that there was no record of her having flown back to Sri Lanka, confirmed that belief. Also, when interviewed, the Appellant gave no explanation for the bones. The rest your Lordship knows.

'A submission of no case to answer in the trial, before Mr Justice Griffiths, thus failed. Doctor Jayasuriya's explanation for the bones, at trial, was that he brought a skeleton from Sri Lanka to use when demonstrating anatomy. Doctor Jayasuriya was convicted by a majority of ten to two of Fathima's murder.'

The Lord Chief Justice intervened: 'Mr Beecroft, you represent the Crown. I assume you agree that this conviction should be overturned?'

'Yes, My Lord,' replied Beecroft.

'Was any check made with the university in Sri Lanka as to whether Doctor Jayasuriya has access to such a skeleton?' asked the Lord Chief Justice.

'Yes, My Lord, but only after Fathima reappeared at the Jayasuriyas' home. It is true, he did have such access.'

'This is extremely distressing,' said the Lord Chief Justice. 'Had this girl not left the Retreat, Doctor Jayasuriya would still be serving life imprisonment. What do you have to say Mr Batty?'

'My Lord, the Home Office agrees that this was a tragedy of errors. What will be of concern is that the jury and the Judge got it completely wrong. Doctor Jayasuriya was, from first to last, innocent and should never have been arrested, tried and convicted.

'It has to be said,' continued Mr Batty. 'That when Doctor Jayasuriya first raised the explanation for the bones, no adjournment was sought either by the prosecution or the defence to check out, in Sri Lanka, Doctor Jayasuriya's explanation.

'Had that happened and there was no sign of Fathima returning to Sri Lanka, Doctor Jayasuriya may well have been acquitted. Equally, had the police conducted a nationwide search in the UK, Fathima would probably have been found. That wasn't done because she had told Doctor Jayasuriya she was flying back to Sri Lanka, which we know was a lie.'

The Lord Chief Justice intervened: 'I think the Home Office

should compensate Doctor Jayasuriya for the injustice he has suffered.'

Mr Batty replied: 'The Home Office agrees, My Lord, and today offers Doctor Jayasuriya one hundred thousand pounds compensation.'

'Thank you, Mr Batty,' said the Lord Chief Justice.

There was a gasp in Court. Turnbull buried his face in his hands.

Doctor Jayasuriya willingly accepted the offer then and there, through his Counsel, Mr Mountfield QC. The appeal was allowed.

The Lord Chief Justice addressed Doctor Jayasuriya: 'The Court is extremely sorry for what has happened. Your appeal against your conviction for murder is allowed and you leave this Court without a stain on your character.

'It is a great pity no evidence was called from Sri Lanka as to whether you had access to a skeleton; nor was any evidence called by either side that Fathima had definitely not returned to Sri Lanka.

'Nor was any search conducted in the UK to see whether Fathima was still here. This case was a tragedy of errors.'

Outside the Court, the press waited for Doctor and Mrs Jayasuriya to come out with their solicitor, Richard Hobson, who read a statement: 'Doctor Jayasuriya is delighted with the outcome. He wants to go home and resume his work as a Lecturer at the Leeds School of Medicine. Please respect his privacy.'

With that, the Jayasuriyas were ushered into a waiting taxi bound for King's Cross railway station.

Chaminda and Tanoo returned to Leeds, treating themselves to first class tickets, thanks to the Home Office. From Leeds, they took the train to Shipley where they were met by a flag-waving crowd. What was odd was that the flag was Sri Lankan.

As soon as they got off the train, the flag-waving crowd rushed towards them. Two press photographers were taking flash photographs. Journalists from the *Yorkshire Post* and Bradford's *Telegraph & Argus* came forward.

'What's it like to be free Doctor Jayasuriya?' he was asked.

'Wonderful,' he replied. 'I just want to put it all behind me now and get on with my life.'

Fiona, the local school teacher, approached them: 'Doctor Jayasuriya, all of us here would like to say how very sorry we are that we didn't believe you. We should have known you would never murder anyone. We feel dreadful and very humbled.'

'Well, that's life,' he said. 'But thank you for your apology. If you'll excuse me, my wife and I just want to go home.'

They walked to the waiting taxi and headed to Baildon and their home.

At the door they were greeted by a smiling Fathima and Venkat who greeted his father with a big hug.

'Welcome home,' they said in unison.

'I've got some food on the go,' said Fathima. 'A Sri Lankan curry which I know is your favourite.'

'How lovely,' said Chaminda. 'But first we must shower and change. It's been a long day and we just want to get out of these clothes.'

Half an hour later, they appeared in the living room, where Fathima had set out some glasses and a plate of spiced spanner crab cutlets, the Sri Lankan canapé which she knew Tanoo made on special occasions.

'Well, this is amazing. I think this calls for a bottle of champagne,' said Chaminda as he headed for the kitchen and returned with a bottle of Lanson Black Label and three champagne flutes. 'Freedom, when I thought my life was over.'

'And it was all my fault,' said Fathima. 'If I hadn't said I was going home because my mother was ill, none of this would have happened. Please forgive me.'

'You're forgiven, child. It was a perfect storm, but now it's over. I just want to go back to work and forget it.'

'I don't know what to call you. I think Chaminda is best because I call my stepfather Dad. I can't have two dads.'

'Fathima, I'm very happy with Chaminda. I can sense what you've decided to do. You're going back to Sri Lanka, aren't you?'

'Yes, but not until my year is out. Venkat has persuaded me to stay, if that's alright with you?'

'Fathima, that's just fine. And, oh, I want to tell you that I've decided to give the hundred thousand pounds to your Retreat in Plymouth.'

EPILOGUE

Chaminda returned to work, receiving a very warm welcome. There was a note on his desk from the Dean's secretary, asking him to call in the office.

The Dean greeted him warmly and, after pleasantries were exchanged, said: 'I've decided to promote you to Senior Demonstrator in Anatomy, but if you walk off with a skeleton, I'll have you!'

'No danger of that,' said Chaminda. 'That's wonderful and so kind of you. Thank you very much. I am delighted to accept the promotion.'

* * *

Fathima returned to Sri Lanka when her year was up. Her father was waiting for her at home. She threw her arms around him: 'Dad,' she said. 'It's so good to be home.'

'It's good to have you home, my darling girl. God bless you. How much I've missed you,' he said as he held her tightly.

* * *

However, that was by no means the end of the matter.

The newspapers which had followed the story throughout the trial picked it up again when Jayasuriya's case came before the Court of Appeal.

The *Daily Mail*'s headline was *Why was the jury so wrong?* And the leader read *Chaminda Jayasuriya was convicted by a jury of the murder of his daughter. His defence was that she was still alive. He was right. She turned up alive and well when he was three weeks into his life sentence for her murder.*

Yesterday, the Court of Appeal reversed the conviction. But let us not forget that before 1957, he would have been hanged by now.

How did our jury system fail him? 'I said throughout that she was alive,' he told our reporter. 'Yet no one believed me. I got abusive mail when in prison. I had to be put in the segregation wing for my own safety. I was called the Wop Doctor even though I'm Sri Lankan, not Italian. I had faith in the English system of justice when I came to the UK but not longer. I am a doctor for God's sake, not a murderer.'

The local Member of Parliament is today taking the matter up with the Home Office, asking why no nationwide hunt was made for the girl, Fathima Mylvaganam, who was throughout in a retreat in Plymouth.

Detective Chief Inspector Turnbull, the officer in charge of the case, said that Doctor Jayasuriya claimed she had returned to Sri Lanka. That was what she had told him, so all efforts were concentrated on checking that.

Asked why he had not put out a nationwide appeal in this country, he said: 'It didn't cross our minds.'

Well, the Daily Mail *says it should have crossed his b..... mind! This poor man could have been incarcerated for his whole life if the girl, who decided to leave the retreat, had stayed there where she had no idea her father had been convicted of her murder in her absence.*

The Home Office, as usual, had no comment to make.

The Daily Mail *reports that, thankfully, Doctor Jayasuriya has been compensated for his trial and imprisonment when no crime had been committed.*

* * *

Other newspapers followed suit.

There were questions in the House of Commons of the Home Secretary.

DCI Turnbull said to the press: 'This mistake was partly of his own making. He made no comment to us when interviewed. He raised his defence for the first time when he was in the witness box. The Judge may well have granted the prosecution an adjournment to make enquiries if one had been sought, but no such request was made. And, if made, it wouldn't have led anywhere as she was throughout in this country.

The Times leader read *Is it time for our jury system to go? Chaminda Jayasuriya was convicted of the murder of his daughter, which he did not commit, by a jury at Bradford Crown Court. Juries in the United Kingdom do not have to give reasons for their decision.*

A top UK lawyer, Professor of Jurisprudence at Cambridge University, Professor James, said to the Times: 'There is a strong argument for the abolition of the jury system in the United Kingdom. It is flawed in that the jury is not required to give any reasons for their decision. Yet article 6(1) of the European Convention of Human Rights (ECHR0) guarantees an accused's right to a "fair trial". This right presumes that the Court will give reasons for its decision, yet juries do not give reasons, nor do Magistrates in their Courts. Is it not time for the jury system itself to be challenged in the European Court?'

The argument in favour of the jury system has always been its independence from the state. An accused is tried by his fellow citizens. But who knows what lay behind the jury's thinking in this case?

The Times leader led to many letters. One from the Professor of Law at King's College London read *Doctor Jayasuriya has no right of appeal because his conviction has already been* overturned. But a time will come when someone appeals to the European Court on the basis that the jury system itself is flawed and denies the accused a fair trial. I remember a trial when the directions in law ran to 65 pages. How can a jury follow such complexity? Enough is enough.

Who knows, wrote The Times, Dr Jayasuriya's case may go down in history for raising this issue. Can someone have a fair trial in the 21st century from a jury?

The editorial in The Times read The jury's verdict in Dr Jayasuriya's trial was perfectly understandable. The girl disappeared. The skeleton of a girl of similar age was found buried and hidden in Dr Jayasuriya's house, garden and laboratory. His explanation had been that she had returned to Sri Lanka. Even if no jury system existed and Dr Jayasuriya was tried by a Judge sitting with lay assessors, and he gave those reasons, the chances are that they would also have found him guilty. It could be said that Dr Jayasuriya brought the prosecution upon himself by concealing bones from a skeleton which by chance corresponded exactly with those of the missing girl, in plant pots and buried behind his garage. His explanation the jury were entitled to regard as fanciful.

The problem is that any system which relies on judgements by human beings is flawed because any such judgement is not scientific. It involves the jury's opinion of the evidence which has been called in the trial. The lack of any evidence from Sri Lanka left a gaping hole. But even if there had been, would the verdict have been any different? There are bound to be mistakes. Churchill said "One man one vote is flawed" but no one has come up with a better idea. Does not the same apply to the jury system?

* * *

Turnbull was distraught at the way the case had gone in the Court of Appeal. He blamed himself for the possible miscarriage of justice. He felt it was his fault for not putting out posters in the UK reporting Fathima as a missing person. It was elementary police procedure and he hadn't followed it. He would be fifty-three next year. Maybe it was time to retire.

He wrote to Bob Illingworth:

Dear Sir,

I have decided, in the light of all that has happened in the trial of Dr Jayasuriya, to tender my resignation with immediate effect.

Yours faithfully,
James Turnbull

* * *

Bob Illingworth called Turnbull and his team together for a meeting in the boardroom at Bradford HQ. Surprisingly, coffee and biscuits were already set out on the table. *What's this about, another bollocking?* thought Turnbull.

Illingworth greeted them all and, when they were seated, said: 'I've called you here in the aftermath of the *missing au pair* case. I know you feel bad about it because we got it wrong. Believe me, you have nothing to reproach yourselves for. You did your duty without any sleight of hand.

'The jury convicted and on that evidence, any jury would have convicted. The jury system is not infallible. None of us is infallible. Mistakes will happen.

'So it is not the time to reproach yourselves, but perhaps the time to ask what we can learn from it. The big lesson, as I see it, is not to accept what is said to you in all innocence.

'The girl told Doctor Jayasuriya a lie and which we all took in, believing that if she had gone anywhere it was back to Sri Lanka in order to look after her mother. Yet, in reality, the girl went missing in the UK.

'The lesson we should learn for the future is that if a supposed victim goes missing in this country, the first thing we should do is launch a nationwide search her in the UK. If we had done that in this case, the chances are we would have found her. That is what we have learnt.

'Old hands like James Turnbull and I are still learning every day we are on the job. The lesson is, never assume guilt. Always think it possible, in the case of a missing person like this, that this person is still here. If you follow that principle, you can't go far wrong.

'Thank you all for coming. I hope this hasn't sounded patronising as that certainly hasn't been my intention.

'As for your letter, James, I have torn it up. Your offer, which is how I read it, is refused. End of conversation.'

With that, Illingworth left the boardroom.

Turnbull said to the team: 'Get back to work. Maybe we'll get it right next time.'